YORK NOTES

General Editors: Professor A.N. Jeffares (*University of Stirling*) & Professor Suheil Bushrui (*American University of Beirut*)

Gustave Flaubert

MADAME BOVARY

Notes by Alastair B. Duncan

MA, Ph D (ABERDEEN)
Lecturer in French, University of Stirling

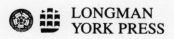
**LONGMAN
YORK PRESS**

NCH : PA

YORK PRESS
Immeuble Esseily, Place Riad Solh, Beirut.

LONGMAN GROUP UK LIMITED
Longman House,
Burnt Mill,
Harlow,
Essex

First published in 1989

ISBN 0-582-95701-X

Typeset by Boldface Typesetters, London EC1
Produced by Longman Group (FE) Ltd
Printed in Hong Kong

Contents

Contents

Part 1

Introduction

GUSTAVE FLAUBERT is one of the greatest French novelists of the nineteenth century. Compared to Balzac or Zola he wrote very few novels* and of these only a handful are now read. *Madame Bovary* is the most well known of these. More successfully here than anywhere else, Flaubert poured much of himself into a novel. This ordinary story about ordinary people is also his own story, set at a distance from himself. Emma Bovary shares Flaubert's desires and frustrations, but her desires are also seen as her weaknesses. We are invited to laugh at her as well as to sympathise with her. Flaubert's bitter hatred of his contemporaries is cleansed in great gusts of laughter; his taste for exaggeration is given healthy scope in satire and caricature; his pessimism is relieved by compassion. What is more, Flaubert differs from many other nineteenth-century novelists in that he largely refrains from telling his readers what to think about his characters. Reading *Madame Bovary* is an adventure in which every reader is invited to construct his or her own version of the story. The more one knows about Flaubert's life and times, the more richly ambiguous the novel becomes.

Flaubert's life and times

Throughout his life Flaubert hated bourgeois ways of thinking and behaving: in *Madame Bovary* he parodied some of them in the figure of Homais, the chemist. Yet he was born in 1821 into a highly respectable bourgeois family, and in many ways lived the life of a typical bourgeois of his time. His father, an admired and respected figure, was the chief surgeon of a hospital in Rouen, the capital of Normandy. Some of his traits appear in the character of Dr Larivière who is called from Rouen to Emma's deathbed. Although the family was wealthy enough, so that Flaubert never had to earn his living, it was expected that he would do so. His elder brother became a surgeon and eventually succeeded to his father's post. Gustave was sent to the Collège Royal in Rouen where his best subjects were French and History. A year after leaving school, he registered as a law student in Paris. From 1842 to 1844 he was supposed to

---

* In *La Comédie humaine*, Honoré de Balzac (1799–1850) grouped together more than a hundred of his novels and tales. Emile Zola (1840–1902) told the story of five generations of the same family in the twenty novels of *Les Rougon-Macquart*.

be studying law but did so without enthusiasm. Then in January 1844 he suffered some kind of nervous attack, possibly a form of epilepsy. He was taken to the family's new home at Croisset on the river Seine outside Rouen and there, slowly, he recovered. The attacks persisted throughout his life, especially at times of stress. There was no question of his pursuing a career. This illness gave him what he wanted — the opportunity to devote his life entirely to literature.

Flaubert had shown literary talent from a very early age. In later life he claimed that he had known *Don Quixote* by heart before he could read. By the age of eight he was writing plays to be performed by his younger sister and their friends. These were, incidentally, the only plays with which Flaubert was ever to gain success. Then he began to write more ambitious narratives: *Passion et Vertu* in 1837, *Smarh* in 1839, *Memoires d'un fou* and *Novembre*, finished in 1842. The titles of the last two give some idea of the mood of these works, none of which was published until long after Flaubert's death. Their passionate heroes and heroines pour out their dreams and aspirations and, above all, their sense of bitter disappointment that life can never live up to an ideal vision, glimpsed but not retained.

These themes were largely inspired by the literature of the time. Emma Bovary read many of the same books, and these will be discussed when we come to look at the novel in more detail. But there were also personal reasons for Flaubert's incapacity to find fulfilment in the present, his longing for an unrealisable ideal. When he was fourteen he fell head over heels in love with Elisa Schlésinger, a married woman with two children and twelve years older than he was. He worshipped her from a distance and never forgot her. In later life, though Flaubert had many relationships with women, some casual, some which lasted for several years, he never married. He lived with his mother until her death in 1872, and no other woman ever took her place in his affections.

How was Flaubert's art to develop beyond the stage of his early romantic outpourings? In *L'Education sentimentale* (1843–5) he began to sketch the outlines of a possible answer. Art should be impersonal. The artist should stand apart from life. He should try to show things as they are, or, in a historical novel, as they were. *La Tentation de Saint Antoine* (1847–9) was his first attempt to put this programme into practice. What could be further from him than the temptations faced by a fourth-century Egyptian monk? But gradually Anthony's experiences came more and more to resemble those of Flaubert. He was tempted not just by the seven deadly sins of Christian mythology, but also by other heresies or vices typically Romantic: pantheism, the belief that God is identical with nature; and *ennui*, a sense that everything has been done and nothing is worth doing. On 12 September 1849 Flaubert finished the work and summoned two friends, Louis Bouilhet (1829–69) and Maxime Du Camp (1822–94), to hear him read it. They listened in silence, then condemned it out of hand. It was, they said, too fantastic, too exotic, too lyrical for contemporary taste. They recommended, so Du Camp claims, that he should write a novel set in the present. This would force him to be less exaggerated, less fantastic.

Almost immediately Flaubert and Du Camp set off on a tour of the Middle East which was to last two years. They visited Egypt, the Red Sea, Palestine, the Lebanon, and came home by way of Greece and Italy. During this time Flaubert conceived a number of projects almost as exotic and remote in time as *La Tentation*. When he returned to Croisset, however, in 1851, the subject he chose to write about was modest, modern and set in his native province of Normandy. It was the story of a doctor's wife, later to become *Madame Bovary*.

For five years Flaubert battled with this subject. He has left a remarkable account of his struggles in the letters he wrote to friends and to his mistress, Louise Colet (1808–76). Progress was slow and painful. He reported that it took him a day to write a page or that he wrote twenty pages in two months. Over and over again he cursed his subject, saying that its bourgeois nature disgusted him or that its vulgarity sometimes made him feel sick. Two convictions spurred him on. He believed first that in art no subject is in itself nobler than another: in his own words, 'Yvetot is worth Constantinople'. (Yvetot is a village in Normandy.) Secondly, he was convinced that the task of the artist is to transform reality and that this transformation takes place as the writer reshapes it in words. Style, then, was all-important for Flaubert. This means, of course, that there was a particular merit in dealing with an apparently flat, ignoble subject. 'To write well about the mediocre' was his aim, and it gave him the impetus to write, scratch out and rewrite his pages time after time until he felt that every image, every sound and every comma was in its appointed place.

In 1856 Flaubert was thirty-four years old, the least distinguished member of a locally prominent medical family. He had published next to nothing, and only a few friends knew that he was an obsessive scribbler. By February 1857 he was the well-known author of a notorious novel which had been praised by the most famous writers of his day and was about to become a best-seller. He owed this change in his fortunes partly to Maxime Du Camp. While Flaubert had worked on his novel, Du Camp had been making a literary career for himself in Paris. As editor of the literary periodical *La Revue de Paris*, he was now true to an old promise and agreed to publish *Madame Bovary* in instalments. Much to Flaubert's rage, however, he insisted on making cuts in the text, largely because he was afraid of the official censor. In fact, a clash with the censors became the main reason for Flaubert's notoriety.

Since 1851 France had been governed autocratically by Louis Napoleon (1808–73), nephew of the great Napoleon (1769–1821). His rule was politically and morally repressive, a repression enforced by strict control of the press. *La Revue de Paris* was a liberal journal and therefore suspect. It may have been partly to suppress it that the imperial prosecutor brought a case against Flaubert and his publisher, accusing them of offending against religion and morality. When the case came to court in January 1857, the prosecutor attacked four parts of the novel in particular: Rodolphe's seduction of Emma, her interest in religion between the two affairs, Léon's seduction, and Emma's death scene. He complained that adultery was lent a poetic charm and that no character condemned Emma. The counsel for the defence asked the judges to take into account the moral of the story: it would dissuade others from adultery by showing them the awfulness of Emma's fate. Of course, it was no part of Flaubert's aim to write a moral fable. But this case, well argued, was enough to persuade the judges. They found that, although in certain passages the novel offended against good taste, it was in essence a work of serious purpose. They acquitted Flaubert, his publisher and his printer of the charges brought against them.

With the success of *Madame Bovary*, Flaubert's life acquired a definitive pattern. In 1855 he had bought himself an apartment in Paris. He now adopted the habit of spending the winter in Paris and retiring to Croisset for the rest of the year. In Paris he did much of the detailed, scholarly reading which underlay all his novels, and he led an active social life. He became friendly with many of the critics and writers who had supported him when *Madame Bovary* was put on trial. In 1863 Princesse Mathilde, a cousin of the Emperor, invited him to attend one of her gatherings of the artistic and social élite. He became a familiar figure in court circles. In 1866, some twenty years after Homais, he was awarded the Legion of Honour.

Flaubert was a large man with a hearty laugh. He enjoyed good food, lively conversation, the company of men and the attentions of women, even if he gave the impression of never being quite at ease in Parisian society. It is a mistake to think of him as an austere, ascetic man or, as legend has it, the hermit of Croisset. Yet there was also that side to his existence, and in creative terms it was perhaps the essential side. He certainly felt it to be so. When he was in residence at Croisset, Flaubert devoted himself, after a morning swim, almost exclusively to writing. It took him almost five years to write *Madame Bovary*. His next novel, *Salammbô*, took a similar amount of time. It is a story set in ancient Carthage and tells how Salammbô, the daughter of Hamilcar, sacrificed herself to help overcome a revolt of mercenary soldiers. Long descriptive passages show Flaubert's desire to be accurate in every historical and archaeological detail, as well as his taste for the exotic, the voluptuous and the cruel. It was his most sustained attempt to evoke a civilisation utterly different from his own and is, as such, an extraordinary achievement. On the whole it was well received when it was published in November 1862.

Flaubert turned next to a modern subject. He had lived most of his conscious life under two forms of government. From 1830 to 1848 France had been ruled by the bourgeois monarch, Louis Philippe (1773–1850), so-called because he had been established on the throne by the upper bourgeois class and because he lived like a member of the bourgeoisie. In 1848 a revolution swept Louis Philippe away, and it appeared briefly that a combination of Liberals and Socialists might establish a new regime favourable to the working class. This coalition, however, broke down in violence in June 1848, and the conservative reaction which followed led eventually to a *coup d'état* by Louis Napoleon in December 1851 and the proclamation of the Second Empire in 1852. This regime lasted until France was invaded and defeated by the Prussian army in 1870.

In *Madame Bovary* Flaubert tells the story of an individual and combines it with a picture of rural French society as it existed at the height of the reign of Louis Philippe. *L'Education sentimentale* combines the same elements, but differently. It is the story of Frédéric Moreau's unfulfilled love for Madame Arnoux, echoing to some extent Flaubert's own relationship with Elisa Schlésinger. It is also the story of a generation of young men who lived through the disappointment of the revolution of 1848. Flaubert portrays most of them as inconsistent and self-interested, lacking will-power and energy. Frédéric is the feeblest of them all. Flaubert worked on this novel between 1864 and 1869. Neither the critics nor the public liked it. It moves very slowly, and many later readers have agreed with the American novelist and critic, Henry James, that it is fatally flawed because it reflects reality through the insipid consciousness of Frédéric.* But other critics and readers regard *L'Education sentimentale* as Flaubert's masterpiece. It binds the personal and the historical together in subtle poetic ways and shows how time almost imperceptibly weaves and unweaves human relationships. Almost all readers agree that the final meeting between Frédéric and Madame Arnoux when both are old and changed is one of the most tender yet ironic scenes in the whole of European literature.

In the final decade of his life between 1870 and 1880 Flaubert suffered much unhappiness. During the war of 1870 Croisset was taken over by Prussian troops. Flaubert hated both the Prussians and the disorder which followed the defeat of France and the fall of the Second Empire. He was also increasingly in financial difficulty. In 1875 he sold almost all his property and gave the proceeds to his niece in order to save her husband from going bankrupt. This was a quixotic act of family loyalty since the money was not nearly enough for the purpose. Above all, perhaps, Flaubert felt that he was growing old, and he missed the many friends who died before him. Louis Bouilhet, on whose literary judgement he had so much relied, died in 1869. His warm friendship and fascinating exchange

---

* Henry James, 'Gustave Flaubert, 1902', in *Selected Literary Criticism*, Heinemann, London, 1963, pp. 212–39.

of letters with the novelist George Sand was ended by her death in 1876. Flaubert's many remaining friends finally persuaded the Government to appoint him to a nominal post on a modest salary of 3,000 francs a year.

Throughout this period Flaubert continued to write. After completing *L'Education sentimentale* he set to work for the third time in his life on a new version of *La Tentation de Saint Antoine*. It was published in 1875 and sold well, though the critics did not like it much. Between 1875 and 1877 he wrote three short stories which were published with the simple title *Trois Contes*. In many ways they sum up Flaubert's genius. 'Un coeur simple' is set in contemporary provincial France. It tells the story of a servant who spends her uneventful life caring for others until one by one they die or leave her; Félicité's life is like an expanded version of that of Catherine Leroux as sketched in the *commices agricoles* scene in *Madame Bovary*. 'La Légende de Saint Julien l'Hospitalier' is the story of a sinner who becomes a saint. Its medieval setting and mystical theme recall *La Tentation de Saint Antoine*. In 'Hérodias', the third tale, Flaubert tries to make an ancient civilisation come to life in all its sensuous, cruel detail, as he did in *Salammbô*. It retells the Bible story of how Salome danced before Herod and how John the Baptist was beheaded.

One other work occupied Flaubert's last years. Throughout his life he had hated clichés. Much of the irony of *Madame Bovary* is directed against those who use language at second hand, whether thoughtlessly, or with malice, or because they can use language no other way. Bouvard and Pécuchet, the heroes of Flaubert's last novel, share Homais's naive belief in human progress. As they explore different fields of human knowledge, they demonstrate, through clichés, the mediocrity of their own minds and, beyond that, the vanity of all knowledge. Yet there is something true about their friendship, and the obsession with note-taking shows that Flaubert could laugh at himself, as he does perhaps also in Binet—the obsessive wood-carver in *Madame Bovary* who resembles his creator, the obsessive carver of words.

Flaubert had just begun the last chapter of *Bouvard et Pécuchet* when he died, suddenly, at Croisset on 8 May 1880.

A note on the text

Madame Bovary was first published in serial form in the *Revue de Paris*. The first instalment was published on 1 October 1856. Many cuts were made in the original text for fear of the official censor. So many more cuts were made than Flaubert had originally agreed, that he wrote a letter of outraged protest to the *Revue de Paris* dissociating himself from the publication. After the successful outcome of the trial, the novel was quickly published in book form by Michel Lévy. It appeared at the end of April 1857. For safety's sake Flaubert had made minor alterations to a few passages, but the text appeared very largely in the form in which he had written it.

The novel was an instant success and has been republished many times in many languages. Most French editions have been based on the last of the five editions to appear in Flaubert's lifetime, but a recent critical edition, published by Flammarion in 1986, is modelled on the fourth edition which has minor variants. Where translations are given in these Notes, they are mostly taken from the Penguin edition, translated by Alan Russell.

Part 2

Summaries
of MADAME BOVARY

A general summary

Charles Bovary, Emma's future husband, is the laughing-stock of his fellow pupils at school in Rouen. With a struggle he eventually passes the examinations to become a medical health officer and sets up a practice in the village of Tostes. When his first wife dies, he quickly finds consolation with Emma Rouault, the daughter of a grateful patient and local farmer. They have an elaborate country wedding, and Charles brings his bride proudly home to his little house and garden in Tostes. He is deliriously happy; Emma finds marriage very disappointing.

Emma's expectations have been raised by reading romantic novels and by the sensual mysticism of her convent education. When she and Charles are invited to a ball at the château La Vaubyessard, this glimpse of what Emma takes to be the glamorous life of the aristocracy increases her dissatisfaction with Charles and Tostes. She falls ill. To restore her health Charles decides to move to another village in Normandy, Yonville-l'Abbaye.

Yonville is dominated by the chemist's shop and its inhabitants by Homais the chemist. On the evening of their arrival in Yonville, Charles and Emma dine at the *Lion d'or* inn with Homais and with Léon Dupuis, a solicitor's clerk. Léon and Emma discover they have tastes in common and they seek refuge in one another's company. Together they visit the house of the wet-nurse who is caring for Berthe, Emma's baby daughter. They spend evenings with Charles and Homais, and they go on an excursion to a flax mill. Emma realises with delight and fear that Léon has fallen in love with her; but when she seeks counsel from the parish priest, Father Bournisien, he misunderstands her and suggests she may be suffering from indigestion. Léon, too timid to declare his love, leaves for Paris, and Emma is plunged into feelings of regret at missing her chance of happiness, and self-pity.

A wealthy local landlord, Rodolphe Boulanger, notices Emma and decides to seduce her. On a day when the attention of all Yonville is centred on the annual agricultural show, Rodolphe woos Emma with romantic clichés. Some weeks later he takes her riding in the forest and she becomes his mistress. Emma at last feels she is living the passionate life of a romantic heroine; but as Rodolphe becomes less attentive, she turns back to Charles. Abetted by Homais, she encourages him to operate on Hippolyte, the stable-boy at the *Lion d'or*, to cure his club foot. The operation is a disaster. Emma is humiliated and furious with Charles. She begins to spend money lavishly and tries to persuade Rodolphe to take her away from Yonville. Her illusions are crushed when at the last moment Rodolphe sends her a callous letter of farewell and leaves without her. Emma thinks of committing suicide. She falls seriously ill. To help to pay for her treatment, Charles, like Emma before him, borrows money from Lheureux, the draper. He also takes her to Rouen to see Donizetti's opera, *Lucy of Lammermoor*. Emma's spirits soar with those of the heroine; she imagines herself setting off with the leading tenor to start a new life. During the interval Charles reintroduces her to an old friend he has just bumped into: Léon.

Léon has returned from Paris a man of the world—in his own eyes at least. Emma refuses to meet him privately at the cathedral in Rouen, but changes her mind. Despite the persistent attentions of a cathedral guide, Léon manages to bundle Emma into a taxi cab, and in this makeshift boudoir they traverse and retraverse the streets of Rouen. Emma finds a pretext to honeymoon for three days with Léon in Rouen and thereafter to return there once a week, ostensibly for piano lessons. (The locals of Yonville admire greatly how much her piano playing improves.) Léon, however, becomes more and more frightened by the single-minded recklessness of her love; and Emma too, after a night at a masked ball, is horrified at the company she is keeping. Meanwhile Lheureux is closing in on Emma. Having encouraged her to borrow more and more, he now demands immediate payment of 8,000 francs. Emma appeals for help to Léon; to the neighbours, Guillaumin, the solicitor, and Binet, the tax collector; and finally to Rodolphe, who has just returned to Yonville. They all turn her down. She goes straight to Homais's store cupboard and poisons herself with arsenic. Grieving and helpless, Charles sends for Dr Canivet from Neufchâtel and Professor Larivière from Rouen. They arrive too late. As Emma dies in agony, Homais invites Larivière to dinner and the villagers take advantage of his presence to consult him about minor or imagined ailments.

At the wake Father Bournisien and Homais, the freethinker, bicker and fall asleep over Emma's corpse. Charles orders a lavish funeral. He never recovers from the blow of Emma's death: he quarrels with his mother and neglects his practice. When he discovers the letters which Emma had received from Léon and Rodolphe, he bears no grudge against them but blames it all on fate. One day Berthe finds him dead in the garden. Lheureux and Homais continue to prosper: Homais is awarded the Legion of Honour.

Detailed summaries

Part I, Chapter 1

A pupil recalls the arrival of a new boy. He had the look of a country bumpkin, and the other boys laughed at him because of his unshapely hat and the timid way he stuttered his name which came out as *Charbovari*.

Charles's father was an assistant surgeon in the army who had retired to the country and ran his farm badly. His mother had transferred all her hopes and ambitions to Charles. At odd moments the village priest taught him Latin. Later he was taken away from school to study medicine. Although Charles preferred to dream and laze, he passed his final exams at the second attempt. His mother set him up in a practice in the village of Tostes and married him to a wealthy widow who plagued him with her jealousy.

NOTES AND GLOSSARY:

Nous étions à l'Etude: 'We were at preparation'. The novel begins as if it is to be told by someone who knew Charles as a boy. In fact, Flaubert uses this narrator very briefly to give an impression of how Charles appears to other people, as clumsy, ill at ease and dim-witted

ridiculus sum: (*Latin*) 'I am ridiculous'. Charles is forced to sum up his behaviour in the opening scene. In these few pages Flaubert shows us what Charles is like and what other people think of him, not by telling us about his character, but by showing him in action

l'*Angelus*: 'Angelus', an evening prayer. The church bell was rung before it, signalling the end of the working day in the French countryside

le retirèrent du collège pour lui faire étudier la médicine: 'took him away from school to study medicine'. Charles is going to be trained as a medical health officer. The training was much shorter and less rigorous than that of a fully qualified doctor, but he would be more skilled than his father whose main qualification was probably the strength to hold a patient down while the army surgeon operated on him

une ignoble petite Venise: 'a sort of shabby little Venice'. In his daydream Charles is endowing Rouen with all the exotic splendour of Venice. The word 'ignoble' brings us back down to earth and points out how far the reality is removed from this dream. This kind of contrast will be one of the main themes of the novel

Part I, Chapter 2

Charles is called out late at night to attend a farmer who has broken his leg. He is much struck by the appearance of the farmer's daughter and returns to the farm more frequently than the case demands. His wife becomes suspicious of these visits, all the more so when she learns that Emma Rouault has been educated and wears fine clothes. She makes Charles promise never to visit the farm again. But shortly afterwards it turns out that Héloïse, Charles's wife, is not to inherit a large sum of money from her previous marriage. She quarrels with Charles's parents, and dies. Charles mourns for her, briefly. 'Elle l'avait aimé, après tout' (She had loved him, after all).

NOTES AND GLOSSARY:

Charles fut surpris de la blancheur de ses ongles: 'Charles was astonished at the whiteness of her nails'. Like Charles in Chapter 1, Emma is first seen from an external point of view. The effect she has on Charles emerges from the way she is described rather than from any explicit comment. Flaubert does not say that Charles finds Emma very attractive, that he thinks she seems refined and superior to her surroundings; but the description of her fingernails and other physical details suggest this

Part I, Chapter 3

Monsieur Rouault consoles Charles about his wife's death and urges him to visit the farm and his daughter. Charles studies Emma intently and cannot get her out of his mind. It occurs to Monsieur Rouault that Charles will make an acceptable if not an ideal match for his daughter. When Charles falteringly requests her hand, Monsieur Rouault transmits the message to Emma. By opening a shutter, he signals to Charles that he has been accepted. The marriage is to take place later, in the spring, when Charles will be out of mourning.

NOTES AND GLOSSARY:

'J'ai été comme vous, moi aussi': 'I've been through it too'. Monsieur Rouault's account of how he suffered when his wife died is comic and moving. His down-to-earth imagery contrasts humorously with his grand theatrical actions, but does not cancel a sense of the farmer's genuine grief

Part I, Chapter 4

The wedding guests arrive in all kinds of carriages and in their varied finery. They parade to the mayor's office and to the church; they eat and drink copiously. Monsieur Rouault stops a cousin playing tricks on the bride and groom. The next morning Charles seems overwhelmed by the experience of the wedding night. Monsieur Rouault sees Charles and Emma off and nostalgically recollects his own wedding.

NOTES AND GLOSSARY:

un mareyeur de leurs cousins—qui même avait apporté, comme présent de noces, une paire de soles: 'a fishmonger cousin—the one who had brought a pair of soles as a wedding present'. This unlikely gift illustrates Flaubert's method. It is quite probable that Flaubert knew of someone who had indeed brought a pair of fish to a wedding. It is the kind of detail he loved. Each detail comes from the real world, but when added together these details make for a vivid vulgarity which verges on caricature

Part I, Chapter 5

Emma explores the tiny, cluttered house and garden at Tostes. In the bedroom she catches a glimpse of the first Madame Bovary's bridal bouquet, which Charles belatedly removes. Charles adores his wife; never has he been so happy; he pursues her with kisses. Emma finds marriage disappointing.

NOTES AND GLOSSARY:

Avant qu'elle se mariât, elle avait cru avoir de l'amour: 'Before the wedding she had believed herself to be in love'. It is a shock for the reader to learn that Emma is dissatisfied with marriage. Flaubert increases the shock effect by setting it immediately after the long description of Charles's happiness. This also conveys how blind Charles is: he would not be so happy if he knew what Emma is thinking. Throughout the novel there is a double irony in the relationship between these two characters. Charles never knows what Emma is thinking; equally Emma herself never grasps that Charles loves her with the passion that she vainly seeks elsewhere

Part I, Chapter 6

From the age of thirteen Emma had been educated in a convent school. The atmosphere of the convent, the books she read there and the stories she was told, inspired in her dreams 'to which the common soul never aspires'.

NOTES AND GLOSSARY:

Paul et Virginie: a popular romance by Bernardin de Saint-Pierre (1787). It describes the innocent love of two fatherless children in the exotic setting of Mauritius

Mlle de La Vallière: a mistress of King Louis XIV who ended her life in a convent

Le Génie du Christianisme: *The Christian Spirit* (1802), a work by the pre-romantic writer Chateaubriand (1768–1848) which defends Christianity on the grounds of its poetic and moral beauty. Christianity is beautiful and it makes you feel good, therefore it is true. Chateaubriand defends this thesis mainly in philosophical reflections about art and literature, but also by illustrating it in the short novels *Atala* (1801) and *René* (1805)

Walter Scott: Scottish writer of vivid historical novels (1771–1832)

Marie Stuart: Mary Queen of Scots, a fiery and passionate Queen of Scotland (1542–87) who was eventually driven from her throne. She was executed by her cousin, Queen Elizabeth of England. The following list of names and events from French history similarly combines the motifs of passion, violence and tragic drama. Flaubert is emphasising Emma's lack of discrimination. All these bits and pieces of history are stored in her mind and feed her imagination

Elle se laissa donc glisser dans les méandres lamartiniens: 'And so she drifted off down the meandering ways of Lamartine'. Alphonse de Lamartine (1790–1869) was a Romantic poet. The phrases which follow in this sentence parody some of the themes of Lamartine's poems: death, loss, the passing of time, and the consolation to be found in nature and religion. Two of his most famous poems are called 'Le Lac' and 'Le Vallon'

Part I, Chapter 7

Emma bitterly compares her present life with what she thinks married life ought to be. Her dull routine makes her resent the happiness Charles finds in her company and the pride he takes in her accomplishments. Charles's mother disapproves of how much money Emma spends on the household and is jealous of Emma's hold on her son. Emma goes walking in the countryside with her dog; but the scene is always the same: she is bored, she misses the happiness of her youth. Then 'quelque chose d'extra-ordinaire tomba dans sa vie' (something quite exceptional befell her). Charles and Emma are invited by the Marquis of Andervilliers to a ball at the château La Vaubyessard.

NOTES AND GLOSSARY:

il eût fallu, sans doute, s'en aller vers ces pays à noms sonores: 'it would doubtless have been necessary to sail away to those lands with musical names'. Emma associates happiness with exotic settings. This is one effect of her reading. She has fallen prey to a belief in the romance of travel and distant lands

Part I, Chapter 8

Emma and Charles arrive at the imposing grounds and château La Vaubyessard. Emma is impressed by the portrait gallery of the Marquis's ancestors and by the Marchioness's gracious greeting. A sumptuous dinner is served at which Emma feasts her eyes on the old Duke of Laverdière. As they dress for dinner Emma forbids Charles to dance. Emma dances. She admires the dresses and the aristocratic men, overhears snatches of a conversation about horse-racing, and glimpses the exchange of a *billet-doux*. Late at night, after supper, Emma waltzes with a Viscount; they turn and turn until she almost swoons. When they retire for the night, Charles is exhausted and goes straight to sleep; Emma tries to stay awake to savour the experience. After breakfast they visit the hothouse and the stables. On the way home Charles picks up a cigar-case dropped by one of the aristo-cratic guests. When they arrive, their meagre supper is not ready. Charles chokes over a cigar. The next day Emma walks miserably up and down her tiny garden looking at her familiar surroundings.

NOTES AND GLOSSARY:

Emma vit autour du jeu des hommes à figure grave: 'Emma saw a group of dignified-looking men standing around the billiard table'. From this point onwards in the chapter, events are seen, explicitly or implicitly, from Emma's point of view. Flaubert arranges every detail to contrast with Emma's life at Tostes: the beautiful garden, the splendid meals, the well-trained servants, the elegant dancing partner. This experience makes

Emma believe that the real world can correspond to what she has read and dreamed about

Marie-Antoinette: wife of King Louis XVI, executed after the Revolution of 1789. Emma is lost in admiration for the old Duke of Laverdière. He seems to her to have led exactly the kind of exciting, unconventional, passionate life which she has read about and which she dreams of for herself. But is the Duke really such an admirable figure? Look closely at how he is described. Over and over again in this chapter Flaubert hints that these people are not nearly as ideal as Emma thinks they are. He is critical of them and to some extent critical of Emma for being taken in by them

leurs jambes entraient l'une dans l'autre: 'their legs intertwined'. This was one of the phrases cut out of the text when it was first published as a serial in the *Revue de Paris*. It was felt to be too shocking. The waltz itself was thought to be a very shocking dance when it swept through Europe in the early nineteenth century — a man and a woman dancing face to face! Flaubert takes advantage of this to turn it into a peak of sensual experience in Emma's life

---

Part I, Chapter 9

Emma remembers the Viscount and dreams of Paris. She employs a new maid and makes an effort to be fashionable and elegant. Charles is doing well, largely by prescribing nothing stronger than sedatives. Emma despises his lack of ambition. Time passes as Emma waits in vain for something to happen. She gives up playing the piano and reading, and wanders on winter days in the garden. From her window she watches the unchanging round of street-life in Tostes. Sometimes a barrel-organ with tiny waltzing figures sends her into a melancholy dream. She begins to neglect the household and becomes capricious and irritable. Charles takes her to a doctor in Rouen who diagnoses a nervous illness and prescribes a change of air. Charles regretfully resolves to leave Tostes. One day, just before they go, Emma throws her bridal bouquet into the fire and watches it burn. She is pregnant.

NOTES AND GLOSSARY:

Marjolaine: a folk song. A peasant girl tells three officers who are courting her that the king's son has given her a bouquet of marjoram: if it flowers, she will be queen.

Emma also has romantic and social aspirations which seem unlikely to be fulfilled. This chapter is a recital of Emma's frustrations, which are all the greater since the false hopes raised by the visit to Vaubyessard. It deals not with a single incident but a lengthy period of time. Notice in how many ways Flaubert conveys Emma's round of never-varying events, for example by the predominant use of the imperfect tense

Eugène Sue: French novelist (1804–57), most famous for his dramatic and sensational novels about life in Paris, published in the 1840s. Emma believes she is reading about life as it actually is

Balzac: Honoré de Balzac (1799–1850), novelist. Many of the volumes of Balzac's famous work, *La Comédie humaine*, are set in Paris; they make it seem an extraordinary and exciting place

George Sand: another contemporary novelist, pen-name of Lucile-Aurore Dupin (1804–76). Paris does not play a large part in her novels, but passion does, and the right of the individual to defy convention and follow the dictates of his or (more often) her heart

Part II, Chapter 1

The village of Yonville-l'Abbaye is set in nondescript agricultural countryside. It has little history and, despite a new road, has seen little progress. Apart from the lawyer's house, the church and the town hall, the most eye-catching building is the chemist's shop. The grave-keeper grows potatoes in an unused part of the cemetery.

Madame Lefrançois, the landlady of the *Lion d'or*, chats with Homais, the chemist, as she prepares for a busy evening. Binet, the local collector of taxes, a silent, solitary man of fixed habits, arrives punctually at six o'clock for supper. The village priest calls to collect his umbrella; Homais seizes the opportunity verbally to attack the church. At last Charles and Emma arrive on the stage-coach, very late, because, to Emma's distress, her pet greyhound had jumped out and been lost.

NOTES AND GLOSSARY:

'monter une poule patriotique pour la Pologne ou les inondés de Lyon': 'put on a tournament in aid of Poland or the flood victims at Lyon'. These are a couple of the references which make it possible to date the events of the novel approximately. Throughout the 1830s and early 1840s there was a great deal of sympathy in France for the victims of the unsuccessful uprising in Poland in 1830. Lyon had disastrous floods in 1840. On the whole, Flaubert avoids giving specific dates. He is concerned with a social climate, rather than with historical accuracy. Here he wants to show Homais's insistence on being up to date

'Mon Dieu, à moi, c'est le Dieu de Socrate, de Franklin, de Voltaire, et de Béranger!': 'My God is the God of Socrates, Franklin, Voltaire and Béranger!' By this Homais means, broadly speaking, that he believes in the existence of a benevolent God, but not in Christianity as revealed in history and organised in the Church. But his list of heroes represents a jumble of names and ideas. Socrates was a Greek philosopher of the fifth century BC; Benjamin Franklin (1706–90) an American inventor, statesman and signatory of the American Declaration of Independence; Voltaire, a French philosopher, writer and satirist (1694–1778); Pierre-Jean Béranger, a satirical poet and song-writer (1780–1857). This list illustrates Homais's pretentiousness. To bring it to a climax with Béranger also shows his lack of discrimination. Béranger was an extremely popular poet in the early nineteenth century but not a man whom Flaubert would regard as an equal of the other three

***Profession de foi du vicaire savoyard*:** 'Savoyard Curate's Profession of Faith'. Part of Jean-Jacques Rousseau's *Emile* (1762) in which he argues that there is a benevolent God whom we can know through the use of reason, and that human beings have an innate sense of justice and virtue

'les immortels principes de 89': 'the immortal principles of the French Revolution of 1789'. Of minimal relevance to the point at issue: Homais is being carried away by his own rhetoric

---

Part II, Chapter 2

Emma and Charles dine with Homais and Léon Dupuis, the local solicitor's clerk, at the *Lion d'or*. Homais discourses in pseudo-learned fashion about the local inhabitants, the weather and the merits of the doctor's house. Léon and Emma conduct a contrasting conversation about the joys of travel, nature, music and reading.

NOTES AND GLOSSARY:
Delille: a mediocre French poet (1738–1813)
*l'Echo des Feuilletons***:** *The Literary Echo.* This is an imaginary periodical. In Homais's list of 'best authors', the great—
Voltaire, Rousseau, Scott—are mixed with the
nondescript. *L'Echo des Feuilletons* is a poor climax
to the list, but it enables Homais to boast that he is the
local correspondent for *Le Fanal de Rouen* (*The
Rouen Beacon*), another fictitious newspaper
invented by Flaubert

Part II, Chapter 3

The characters react to the arrival of Charles and Emma in Yonville.
Emma is a breath of fresh air in Léon's dull existence. Homais acts the
good neighbour: he has treated patients, which as a chemist he is not
legally permitted to do, and he wants to make sure that Charles will not
reveal this to the authorities. Charles has few patients and little money but
delights in his wife's pregnancy. Emma longs for a son; she gives birth to a
daughter, Berthe. Charles's parents come for the baptism, and his father
dazzles Emma with stories of his licentious lifestyle.

Léon accompanies Emma on a walk out of the village to visit Berthe,
who is in the care of a wet-nurse, Madame Rollet. They are idyllically
happy but repeatedly brought down to earth: Berthe is sick over Emma,
Madame Rollet demands more money.

Léon reflects that only Madame Bovary can save him from boredom, but
she seems inaccessible.

NOTES AND GLOSSARY:
On parcourut le calendrier: 'They went through the church calendar'.
According to French law, children had to be named
after a saint to be found in the official church calendar
of saints' days. Fortunately there are a great number
of saints, known and unknown, although the calendar
probably did not contain some of the exotic names
which Emma would have preferred. The name
Madeleine would be in the calendar. It is derived from
Mary Magdalene, one of the first followers of Jesus,
who is traditionally thought to have been a prostitute
*Athalie***:** a tragic drama by the classical French dramatist, Jean
Racine (1639–99). It has a biblical theme and strong
Christian sympathy. This explains Homais's comic
anguish: he wants to approve of Racine artistically but
has to condemn his philosophy. There is strong irony

in Flaubert's comment about Homais: 'le penseur chez lui n'étouffait point l'homme sensible' (the thinker never stifled the man of feeling). We have already seen enough of Homais to know that he is neither thinker nor man of feeling

Le Dieu des bonnes gens: 'The God of Good People'. A song by Béranger. According to the song, the good people's God is on the whole benevolent and a supporter of Napoleon (which is why he would appeal to the ex-Napoleonic soldier, Monsieur Bovary). He wants to have nothing to do with the monarchy restored in 1814, or with the priests who came with it

La Guerre des dieux: *The War of the Gods*. A work by the poet Evariste-Désiré de Parny (1753–1814). No doubt Monsieur Bovary senior quotes an anti-clerical passage

Mathieu Laensberg: a popular almanac which hawkers sold from door to door in country districts

Part II, Chapter 4

Emma's life at Yonville falls into a routine. Homais calls on the Bovarys at supper; they return the visit and play cards with him in the evening. Emma and Léon are becoming more involved with one another. They chat and whisper together while Charles and Homais play dominoes. They exchange favours and presents. Léon cannot find a way to declare his love; Emma has not realised what is happening.

NOTES AND GLOSSARY:

une belle tête phrénologique: 'a fine phrenological head'. Phrenology: a pseudo-science which claimed there was a correlation between mental characteristics and the shape of the skull. With this present Léon is paying a somewhat dubious homage to Charles's supposed scientific interests

Part II, Chapter 5

As Homais conducts a guided tour of a flax-mill, Emma compares Léon with Charles. She realises that she and Léon are in love. To all appearances she remains virtuous. She resists the attempts of Lheureux to sell her finery and knick-knacks and to lend her money. She receives Léon coolly, and acts the part of the perfect wife and mother, to the admiration of Charles and the people of Yonville. Inwardly, she rages against the frustrations of her life, and especially against Charles.

NOTES AND GLOSSARY:

Rien pourtant n'était moins curieux que cette curiosité: 'Nothing could have been less interesting than this object of interest'. The dullness of this winter visit to a half-built factory heightens the reader's sympathy for Emma and makes Homais's enthusiasm all the more comic. Flaubert had little time for the achievements of modern industrial civilisation

Né Gascon, mais devenu Normand: 'Gascon by birth and Norman by choice'. Traditionally, people from Gascony are said to be boastful and vain, while Normans are shrewd and tight-fisted. These first comments about Lheureux begin to paint an unpleasant picture

Trois Frères, Barbe d'Or, Grand Sauvage: 'Three Brothers, Golden Beard, Great Savage'. Fashionable drapers' shops in Rouen, at least one of which, *la Barbe d'Or*, actually existed

Sachette de *Notre-Dame de Paris*: in fact, Paquette de Chantefleurie, mother of the heroine of Victor Hugo's novel *Notre-Dame de Paris* (1831). Her daughter had been stolen from her as a tiny baby and is restored to her in the course of the novel.

Part II, Chapter 6

The evening bells in spring make Emma recall her youth. She goes to church and tries to tell the priest, Bournisien, about her suffering. Bournisien cannot understand her because he can only conceive of suffering in its most obvious physical or social forms. In any case he is preoccupied with the boys of the village as they gather for their religious instruction class. Emma goes home and, in frustrated rage, knocks Berthe to the ground. She conceals how this happened; Charles consoles her; and Homais moralises about the dangers of accidents to children.

Léon, tired of making no progress with Madame Bovary, resolves to leave for Paris. He calls on Emma to say a stilted goodbye. That same evening Homais visits the Bovarys as usual. Charles is concerned about how Léon will survive in Paris. To Emma's secret distress, Homais paints a vivid picture of the excitement and dangers the capital holds in store for a young man. He confides the great news that the regional agricultural show may be held in Yonville that year.

NOTES AND GLOSSARY:

elle entendit tout à coup sonner l'*Angelus*: 'she suddenly heard the chimes of the Angelus'. The Angelus bell was supposed to be rung at sunset. Lestiboudois rings it earlier, at a time which suits him. This hints at a theme which runs through this chapter: religious practice in Yonville is in no way the expression of a deep, committed spirituality

catéchisme: 'catechism'. A form of religious instruction which consists, strictly, of questions and answers. Flaubert suggests it is practised in this form in Yonville: 'Qu'est-ce qu'un chrétien? — C'est celui qui, étant baptisé . . . , baptisé . . . , baptisé' (What is a Christian? — A Christian is one who, being baptised . . . being baptised . . . being baptised). The repetition suggests that the boys are simply reciting by rote, rather than understanding what they are saying

l'enfle: 'swollen belly'. A typical Norman expression; standard French would be *enflure*. Bournisien is conscientious and hard-working, irreproachable within his limitations. But when Emma asks him whether he relieves all miseries — thinking of her own — his mind jumps to the welfare of cows

'des Caraïbes ou des Botocudos': 'Caribs or Botocudos'. Native peoples of the West Indies and South America. In scolding his wife for being too protective of their children, Homais is showing off his anthropological knowledge

---

Part II, Chapter 7

Emma bitterly regrets having let Léon go. She has sudden fits of energy and spends money freely, but nothing seems of value to her. Charles is greatly concerned and consults his mother, who recommends that Emma's supply of novels should be cut off. On the day Charles's mother leaves Yonville, a busy market day, Emma is watching the crowds from her window and sees a peasant and his master approaching the house. The peasant wants to be bled. Both he and Justin, Homais's assistant, faint at the sight of the blood. Charles summons Emma to help him. Her looks and the movement of her dress make an impression on the peasant's master, Rodolphe Boulanger of La Huchette. As he walks home Rodolphe thinks about Emma: she is probably bored and would make a charming mistress. He decides to seduce her at the agricultural show.

Part II, Chapter 8

On the morning of the agricultural show the militia and the fire brigade parade in the decorated streets, and visitors throng into Yonville. Only

Madame Lefrançois, the innkeeper, is unhappy because the important guests are to dine in a marquee, not at the *Lion d'or*. She is surprised to learn that Homais is going to join them. He explains his interest by giving her a lecture on the relevance of chemistry to agronomy. Emma is out walking, leaning on Rodolphe's arm. Rodolphe gives the slip to Homais and Lheureux and hints to Emma that he is in love. They pass by the field where the animals are tethered, and Rodolphe begins to make fun of the show and the stifling dullness of life in the country. He laments the melancholy solitude of his own existence. An official from the prefecture greeted by a guard of honour and by the mayor, Monsieur Tuvache. While the official party take their places on the platform, Lheureux and Homais grumble that the decorations are not grand enough. Emma and Rodolphe make their way up to the council chamber of the town hall from where they can see but not be seen.

The narrative now splits into two strands. The events of the show are interspersed with the account of Rodolphe's seduction of Emma. The Prefect's representative, Monsieur Lieuvain, gives a speech which presents an idealised picture of the King, the Government and the place of farmers and farming in national life. Meanwhile Rodolphe is presenting to Madame Bovary an idealised image of himself as a man dissatisfied by life, who longs for a soul-mate with whom to share a passionate existence, far superior to the conventions of society.

The people of Yonville are listening intently to Monsieur Lieuvain's speech; Emma relaxes into drowsy recollections of Vaubyessard and Léon.

The narrative cuts ever more rapidly from one scene to the other. The chairman of the show announces the prizewinners as Rodolphe declares his love and presses Emma's hand, which she does not withdraw.

A silver medal and twenty-five francs are presented to Catherine Leroux for fifty-four years of faithful service.

At the banquet Rodolphe is lost in thoughts of Emma. The firework display does not succeed; Homais fusses about the risk of fire; Binet, who commands the fire brigade, reacts sharply to Homais's interfering comments. Rodolphe, in Emma's hearing, agrees with Madame Homais that it has been a lovely day.

Two days later the *Fanal de Rouen* publishes a glowing account of the show written by Homais.

NOTES AND GLOSSARY:

M. le préfet: 'the Prefect'. A government official in charge of a Department, a large administrative region. The Prefect does not come to the show but sends a minor official to represent him. This humorously undermines Monsieur Lieuvain's claim that the Government sets a high value on agriculture

des drapeaux tricolores: 'tricolours'. The French flag, associated with the Republican tradition but in use again since the Revolution of 1830 which set Louis-Philippe on the throne

'Plût à Dieu que nos agriculteurs . . . écoutassent davantage les conseils de la science!': 'Would to heaven our farmers paid more attention to scientific teaching!' This could be written more simply as, 'les paysans devraient prendre en compte les enseignements de la science'. Homais's syntax, especially his use of the past subjunctive, is as grotesquely pompous as his choice of vocabulary. The English rendering misses the full flavour of the French

'C'est Lheureux qui le fait vendre': 'Lheureux's forcing him to sell up'. Lheureux has forced the owner of the *Café Français* to sell up by suddenly insisting that he pays all his bills at once. In the following lines Lheureux is seen bowing to Madame Bovary. Flaubert is signalling that she will be one of his future victims

'Qui n'a souvent réfléchi à toute l'importance que l'on retire de ce modeste animal . . . ?': 'Who has not frequently pondered on the great importance to us of that homely animal . . . ?' The truthful answer is that next to no-one would have pondered on this. Flaubert takes great pleasure in satirising provincial officialdom in the pomposity of this speech. It abounds in absurd rhetorical questions, mixed metaphors and ludicrous circumlocutions. Notice how many words the official uses to describe bread or feathers, but imagination comically deserts him when he gets to eggs

Loyola: Ignatius Loyola (1491–1556), founder of the Jesuit Order of Catholic priests. Anticlerical opinion was strongly opposed to the Jesuits who, it was believed, plotted to take over education and the state. There is comic exaggeration in Homais's labelling Bournisien a follower of Loyola, since the traditional marks of the Jesuit are militancy and intellectual subtlety

Part II, Chapter 9

Rodolphe calculates that absence will make Emma's heart grow fonder. He calls on her six weeks later and claims that, irresistibly, her charms have drawn him back. Charles strongly encourages Emma to accept Rodolphe's invitation to go riding for the sake of her health.

Emma and Rodolphe set off on a misty October day. They dismount in the forest and Rodolphe tells Emma how much he needs her. Emma finally capitulates to him.

That evening Charles announces that he has bought a mare for her. Emma retires to her room and exults in the thought that she has a lover and she will now know all the joys of love.

Rodolphe and Emma meet and write to one another regularly. She gets into the habit of going to his house early in the morning. To begin with, Rodolphe is charmed, but eventually he becomes alarmed that she will be seen.

NOTES AND GLOSSARY:

Charles écrivit à M. Boulanger que sa femme était à sa disposition et qu'il comptait sur sa complaisance: 'Charles wrote to Monsieur Boulanger that his wife awaited his convenience and that they would be most grateful'. The translation loses some of the irony of the original. Charles is literally putting his wife at Rodolphe's disposal; and, as Emma's lover, Rodolphe will soon be counting on the obliging nature of Charles, her husband

Part II, Chapter 10

Emma also begins to worry that her liaison will be discovered. One morning as she returns from La Huchette she encounters Binet, who is duck-shooting. She gives him the unconvincing explanation that she was visiting Berthe, and is further embarrassed to meet him again in the chemist's shop the same evening.

Emma and Rodolphe now organise their *rendez-vous* with more care. When Charles finally falls asleep in the evening, Emma slips out to meet her lover in the chill of the garden or, if it is raining, in Charles's surgery. Rodolphe continues to be charmed by Emma's innocence, but is disconcerted by her sentimentality. He grows less effusive; Emma senses the change and clings to him all the more.

A kind and gossipy letter from her father suddenly makes Emma see her childhood as a golden time. It inspires her to take a passing interest in Berthe. Rodolphe remains cool; Emma regrets her liaison.

Part II, Chapter 11

Homais and Emma persuade Charles to operate on the stable-boy Hippolyte's club foot, even though Hippolyte has hopped around happily on it all his life. A box is constructed to enclose the foot. Charles cuts a tendon;

Hippolyte feels no pain. Charles and Emma are celebrating when Homais arrives to read them a fulsome account of the operation destined for the *Fanal de Rouen*.

Five days later Hippolyte is in agony. Three days after that his foot is black. Madame Lefrançois and the customers of the *Lion d'or* try to comfort him; Bournisien beseeches him to repent; all to no avail.

Amid great excitement Dr Canivet arrives from Neufchâtel to amputate Hippolyte's lower leg. He attends first to his horse, then lectures Homais on the robustness of his constitution: Homais has declined to assist him because he is too sensitive.

Charles is skulking at home, while Emma reflects bitterly on how she could ever have imagined that Charles could be up to the operation, or be anything but mediocre. As Hippolyte's screams subside, Charles tries to embrace Emma. She fends him off, and that night throws herself into Rodolphe's arms.

NOTES AND GLOSSARY:

En effet, Bovary pouvait réussir: 'Bovary might, indeed, be successful'. Emma is deceiving herself. Charles is an officer of health, not a fully qualified doctor, far less a surgeon. There was next to no chance he would operate successfully

le volume du docteur Duval: 'Dr Duval's treatise'. V. Duval, *Traité pratique du pied bot* (*A Treatise on the Treatment of Club Foot*). This book was Flaubert's source for much of the technical information used in this chapter. The technical details are meant to be as confusing to Charles as they are to the reader

'C'est comme le strabisme, le chloroforme et la lithotritie, un tas de monstruosités que le gouvernement devrait défendre!': 'It goes with strabismus, and chloroform and lithotrity, a lot of monstrous rubbish that ought to be stopped by the Government!' Canivet is opposed to all new-fangled ideas in medicine whether good or bad. His extreme conservatism provides a comic contrast to Homais's blind belief in progress. Chloroform was first used experimentally as an anesthetic in the 1830s. Lithotrity is an operation which consists of crushing a stone in the bladder so that its fragments can be removed by urinating. It also dates from the 1830s. Strabismus, meaning a squint, has been in use as a medical term since the sixteenth century. What possible objection Canivet could have had against strabismus remains a mystery

Elle se repentait, comme d'un crime, de sa vertu passée: 'She repented of her past virtue as if it were a crime'. This is a key to one of the main functions of this chapter in the novel. It provides the ultimate proof to Emma of Charles's mediocrity, and so encourages her to think of taking the irreversible step of running away with Rodolphe

---

Part II, Chapter 12

Emma suggests to Rodolphe that they should run away together. To please him she dresses beautifully. As a result Lheureux presents her with a large bill which she pays by taking the fees owed to Charles by a patient. Rodolphe, though embarrassed by her extravagant presents and her protestations of love, continues to take advantage of her. Charles's mother is scandalised by Emma's dress and her speech, and criticises Emma to her face. Following this dispute, Emma begs Rodolphe to take her away; he asks what is to become of Berthe.

In her anticipation of leaving Yonville, Emma is at her most beautiful. Charles finds her irresistible. He dreams of a future when Berthe will grow up to be like her mother and settle down happily with some sensible young man. In ironic contrast, Emma dreams of travelling alone with Rodolphe in distant lands. She orders a coat and a trunk from Lheureux. Rodolphe keeps putting off the date of their departure. On a moonlit evening Emma and Rodolphe savour their happiness. Emma expects to leave the next day; Rodolphe goes home regretting that he has got to lose such a pretty mistress.

NOTES AND GLOSSARY:

Amor nel cor: (*Italian*) 'love in the heart'

Il s'était tant de fois entendu dire ces choses, qu'elles n'avaient pour lui rien d'original: 'He had listened to so many speeches of this kind that they no longer made any impression on him'. In this paragraph Flaubert explicitly passes judgement on Rodolphe for not being able to discern true sentiments even when they are poorly expressed. There is an implied defence of Emma here: she has a full heart, as opposed to the shrivelled hearts of Rodolphe and most of the inhabitants of Yonville. The generalisation at the end of the paragraph shows the source of some of Flaubert's sympathy. Emma is often unable to express herself adequately or appropriately, and Flaubert, who took five years to write *Madame Bovary*, knows how difficult the problem can be

comme le duc de Clarence dans son tonneau de malvoisie: 'like the Duke of Clarence in his butt of malmsey'. Shakespeare records in *Richard III* that the Duke of Clarence drowned in a butt of malmsey wine. Flaubert adds a humorous footnote to history by suggesting that he was left to pickle in it

---

Part II, Chapter 13

On arriving home, Rodolphe writes to Emma. He tries to refresh his memory of her by going through a box of love-letters, but Emma fades into the crowd of his discarded lovers. As he writes his farewells, he cynically weighs up the effect that every hackneyed phrase will have upon Emma. His final touch is a drop of water to imitate a tear-drop.

The next day he sends the letter to Emma in a basket of apricots. Emma flees with it to the attic. For a moment she is tempted to throw herself out of the window. At supper Charles remarks that he has heard Rodolphe is leaving Yonville, and he offers Emma an apricot. She faints when Rodolphe passes the window in a carriage. Charles explains to Homais that the fit had taken her while she was eating apricots; Homais discourses on the nasty effects of smells. For forty-three days Emma lies ill with brain fever; Charles never leaves her side.

NOTES AND GLOSSARY:

rien de vert n'y poussait: 'nothing green grew there'. It is typical of Flaubert to pass judgement on Rodolphe by means of an extended image

'*That is the question*': Homais reports that he has read this sentence in a newspaper. He does not realise it is a quotation from Shakespeare's *Hamlet*. Flaubert is having a wry smile at Homais's lack of culture

---

Part II, Chapter 14

Charles is in financial difficulty due to Emma's illness; he borrows heavily from Lheureux. During her convalescence Emma finds sensual and spiritual consolation in religion. She reads religious tracts given her by Bournisien, does charitable works in the village, and even becomes friendly with her respectable neighbours. As she recovers, this phase passes.

One day when Charles, Bournisien, Binet and Homais are drinking cider together, Homais suggests that Charles should take Emma to Rouen to hear the famous tenor, Lagardy. Bournisien is provoked into a dispute with Homais about the Church's attitude to the theatre. Charles persuades

Emma to go. He is excited and confused by the formalities of buying tickets for the performance. They reach the theatre before the doors open.

NOTES AND GLOSSARY:

M. de Maistre: Joseph de Maistre (1753–1821). A moralist and Catholic philosopher who condemned the French Revolution and upheld the authority of king and pope. Notice that Emma is not reading de Maistre himself but only something written in his style. Her other religious reading is similarly second-hand, a hotch-potch of texts about issues which are of no interest to her

Emma, sans doute, ne remarquait pas ses empressements silencieux ni ses timidités: 'His silent eagerness and bashfulness were no doubt lost on Emma'. Justin's adolescent devotion to Emma is a recurrent motif in the novel. Emma is as blind to it as she is to Charles's love. Justin and Charles will be her two genuine mourners

Castigat ridendo mores: (*Latin*) 'It corrects morals by means of laughter'. The motto of comedy

Galilée: Galileo Galilei (1564–1642). A physicist and astronomer who was forced to recant some of his theories by the Catholic Inquisition. It is a cliché to use his name as a symbol of progressive scientific enlightenment in the face of religious conservatism

Part II, Chapter 15

Emma is excited by the elegance of the theatre. She knows the story of the opera because she has read Walter Scott's *The Bride of Lammermoor*. She identifies with the heroine and is captivated by Lagardy. Charles cannot follow the story at all. For a moment the disappointments of Emma's own life make her resist the emotions of the marriage contract scene, but the reappearance of Lagardy soon recaptures her imagination: she sees herself travelling round the world with him. Charles fetches her a glass of water and meets Léon whom he invites to join them in their box. Emma loses herself in memories of Léon. They leave the theatre before the performance ends. In a café Léon talks about the music and musicians he has heard in Paris. Charles suggests that Emma should stay on in Rouen to go to a complete performance of the opera with Léon.

NOTES AND GLOSSARY:

Lucie de Lammermoor: an opera by Donizetti (written 1819, first performance 1835), from the novel *The Bride of*

Lammermoor by Walter Scott. Flaubert follows the action of the opera very closely. Lucy Ashton is in love with Edgar Ravenswood, an enemy of her family. Her brother, Henry Ashton, wants her to marry Lord Arthur Bucklaw. In Act I Ashton, while hunting, is informed about Lucy and Edgar's love by his servant Gilbert. At a fountain in the forest (imitated by a flute), Lucy sings her famous *cavatina*, a short solo song in simple style. Edgar arrives, only to inform her that he is being sent on a mission to France. They swear eternal love and take passionate leave of one another. In Act II Ashton persuades Lucy to marry Bucklaw by showing her a forged letter supposedly written by Edgar, guaranteed by a false engagement ring. Lucy consents to marry Lord Arthur, but has to be half-carried to the contract-signing ceremony. Edgar appears and curses Lucy for betraying him. Act II ends in a sextet conveying in particular the differing emotions of Lucy, Edgar, Ashton and Arthur. After the interval, at the beginning of Act III, the wedding guests learn that Lucy has gone mad and killed her newly-wed husband. Lucy appears, dishevelled and blood-stained, to sing of her lost love in one of the most famous scenes in Romantic opera. She dies. Edgar learns of her death as the funeral cortege passes. He sings of his beloved angel Lucy and kills himself in grief.

Flaubert uses the opera to highlight the different responses his characters have to it. For Emma it is a spring-board for her own thoughts. She loses interest entirely when Léon comes on the scene; or perhaps she does not want to identify herself with the heroine's madness and death? Charles tries patiently to follow what is happening, but gets it all confused: the two characters who walk off arm in arm are not father and lover, as he suggests, but brother and prospective husband. Léon's suggestion that they should leave before the end (so that he can renew acquaintance with Emma) contrasts ironically with the enthusiasm he showed for music when they first met at the *Lion d'or*. Mingling with these points of view is that of the author, who emerges distinctly from the shadows to damn Lagardy—a hero in Emma's eyes—by describing him as 'cette admirable nature de charlatan, où il y avait du coiffeur et du toréador' (this admirable charlatan, part hairdresser, part toreador)

Part III, Chapter 1

The next afternoon Léon visits Emma at her hotel. They recall the past, and each claims to have lived a life of solitary suffering since Léon left Yonville. He tells her that he had loved her; she tells him they must part, but agrees to meet him the next morning in the cathedral and allows him to kiss her. When he goes, Emma writes him a letter to cancel the appointment, but since she does not know the address, decides she will deliver it in person at the cathedral.

The next morning, a fine summer's day, Léon buys flowers and waits for Emma. He curtly dismisses the beadle who wants to show him round. At last Emma arrives, gives him the letter and kneels to pray, without much conviction, for courage to resist him. The beadle approaches Emma who seizes the pretext of visiting the cathedral as a last line of defence. The beadle enthusiastically describes the tombs of long-dead warriors; Emma pretends to be interested; Léon is irritated and discouraged. At last he hustles Emma out of the church, summons a cab and she gets in because, 'cela se fait à Paris' (it's the done thing in Paris). Léon orders the cabby to drive anywhere he likes. Throughout the day the coach is seen all round Rouen. Once an ungloved hand appears beneath the drawn blinds and tosses away some scraps of white paper, no doubt the remains of Emma's letter.

NOTES AND GLOSSARY:

la *Chaumière*:   a Parisian café and ballroom much frequented by students and 'grisettes', the young working-class girls whom they picked up

Il prétendit avoir été guidé vers elle, au hasard, par un instinct. Elle se mit à sourire: 'He pretended he had been guided to her by an instinct. She started smiling'. Emma is not taken in by Léon's words, even if she cannot resist them. She has heard words like them before, used innocently by Léon during their first meeting at the *Lion d'or*, manipulated for his own ends by Rodolphe at the agricultural show. In each of these scenes the characters draw on the same stock of Romantic clichés: the futility and boredom of life, the consolation of nature, the supremacy of feeling, and pre-destined love between man and woman as a value transcending conventional morality

La Tour de Nesle: a popular historical drama (1832) by Alexandre Dumas

Part III, Chapter 2

Emma misses the coach home to Yonville but catches up by hiring a cab. Félicité, her maid, meets her and tells her that Homais has a message for her. Homais is raging at Justin: the apprentice had been sent to fetch a pan for jam and had taken one from Homais's locked storeroom, from directly beside a bottle of arsenic. Justin's disgrace deepens when a book entitled '*L'Amour conjugal*' (*Married Love*) falls out of his pocket. At last Homais turns to Emma and tells her, 'Votre beau-père est mort' (Your father-in-law is dead). Charles had asked Homais to break the news gently.

At supper Charles thinks about his father and mother; Emma thinks how she despises Charles. Charles's mother arrives. She and Charles are plunged in grief; Emma recalls her day with Léon.

Lheureux encourages Emma to put off paying the money Charles owes him, and suggests that Emma should arrange to take charge of all Charles's financial affairs. Emma presses the idea on Charles, who sends her to Rouen to consult Léon about it. She stays there three days.

NOTES AND GLOSSARY:

capharnaüm: a place where things are stored in a jumble. It is typical of Homais's self-importance that he should use a relatively unusual, Latin-sounding word for his storeroom. Flaubert needs this scene for his plot — Emma has to know where she can obtain arsenic to poison herself — but he skilfully turns it into a display of Homais's comic outrage and his insensitivity to others

Fabricando fit faber, age quod agis: (*Latin*) 'The craftsman becomes a craftsman by working at his trade, do what you can do best'

procuration: 'Power of Attorney'. A legal act by which one person is given the authority to take legal and financial decisions for someone else

Part III, Chapter 3

Emma and Léon spend three blissful days together in Rouen; in the evenings they take a boat out on the river.

NOTES AND GLOSSARY:

Deux Robinsons: 'two Robinson Crusoes'. *Robinson Crusoe* (1719) by

Daniel Defoe is the story of a man who was marooned on a tropical island. Here, very briefly, Emma comes close to realising her dream of exotic travel

Un soir, t'en souvient-il? nous voguions: 'One night, do you remember, we were drifting'. A quotation from Lamartine's poem 'Le Lac' in which he recalls past happiness with a lover, now dead. (See also Notes to Part I, Chapter 6)

Adolphe . . . Dodolphe: this reference to Rodolphe reminds Emma with a jolt that love is not always a matter of idyllic happiness

---

Part III, Chapter 4

Léon visits Emma in Yonville. She promises to find a way of coming to Rouen regularly. She begins to play the piano again, badly. It is clear she needs lessons. Charles stifles his worries about the expense and sends her to Rouen for a piano lesson once a week.

NOTES AND GLOSSARY:

'une idée de Rousseau, peut-être un peu neuve encore': 'an idea of Rousseau's, still a bit new perhaps'. Rousseau (1712–1778) put forward the idea that mothers should educate their children themselves in *La Nouvelle Héloïse* (1761) and in *Emile* (1762); Homais is speaking in the 1840s. Flaubert is making fun of how long it takes an idea to reach the provinces

On trouva même, au bout d'un mois, qu'elle avait fait des progrès considérables: 'At the end of the first month, she was thought to have made considerable progress'. More fun at the expense of the provincials, since Emma has, of course, not been to a single lesson— although this will not prevent the piano teacher from sending Charles a bill for the lessons after Emma's death (see Part III, Chapter 11)

Part III, Chapter 5

On Thursdays Emma takes the early morning coach to Rouen. Her intense awareness of countryside and town reflects her rising excitement. She and Léon spend the day in a hotel bedroom, enthralled by one another. In the evening, as the coach climbs the hill out of Rouen, a ragged blind beggar appears at the window and fills Emma with dread. At home, she has nothing to say to Charles; she longs for the next Thursday. One day, while lamenting how fickle men are, Emma almost tells Léon about Rodolphe.

Charles discovers that Mademoiselle Lempereur, the piano teacher, does not know Emma. Emma produces receipts to prove she has had lessons. She begins to take pleasure in inventing lies and subterfuges. She is almost found out by Bournisien; Lheureux sees her and Léon together.

Lheureux presents her with a lengthy bill, persuades her to sell a cottage inherited from old Monsieur Bovary, and then to borrow and spend more money on the proceeds rather than pay off her debts. Some months later Lheureux presents Charles with a fresh bill. Madame Bovary senior is outraged and makes Charles promise to withdraw the Power of Attorney from Emma, but Emma wins it back and drives her mother-in-law out of the house. Emma celebrates this triumph with Léon. She becomes reckless and hurls herself more eagerly on the good things in life. One night she does not come home. Charles searches for her throughout Rouen. She tells him she cannot feel free if he is going to be so upset by the least delay. Now Emma visits Rouen whenever she pleases, makes Léon come to her from his office and generally takes command of his life.

NOTES AND GLOSSARY:

L'odalisque au bain, Femme pâle de Barcelone: *Odalisque bathing, Pale Woman of Barcelona*. Typical titles of Romantic paintings. Léon is a pale copy of Emma. He does not see the real Emma but an image of her, distorted by the vague, idealised figures of Romantic art

Souvent la chaleur d'un beau jour/Fait rêver fillette à l'amour: 'When the sun shines warm above / It turns a maiden's thoughts to love'. The contrast between the beggar's gay song and his horrifying appearance is a symbolic warning of the fate which will overtake Madame Bovary. In this chapter Emma basks in love and dominates Charles and Léon; but Lheureux is already preparing her downfall

Part III, Chapter 6

One Thursday Homais decides to visit Léon in Rouen. He takes him to lunch, then pursues him to the hotel where Emma is waiting, and drags him off to a café. Emma is furious with Léon and thinks of all his bad qualities.

In a despairing attempt to revive her love, she writes him conventional love letters; her embraces become more passionate. Léon takes fright at the violence of her passion: his personality is being absorbed by hers; she wants to know everything about him.

One day Emma passes her old convent school. She wonders why everything she has touched in her life has instantly turned to dust.

A large bill arrives from Monsieur Vinçart, an associate of Lheureux, followed by a threat to seize the Bovarys' furniture and effects. Emma runs to Lheureux who extends her credit on the strength of some money still due from the sale of the cottage. She continues to stave off Lheureux by extracting payment from Charles's patients and borrowing from her neighbours.

Charles attributes Emma's short temper to a recurrence of her illness. He wanders alone with Berthe in the neglected garden. Emma stays in her room, reads novels full of 'tableaux orgiaques avec des situations sanglantes' (blood and orgies), and lusts for her next meeting with Léon.

When Emma asks Léon to pawn six spoons for her, he begins to reflect that perhaps his mother and his employer have been right in pressing him to give her up. Both Emma and Léon are now weary of the relationship but do not know how to end it. She accompanies him to a masked ball; in the morning she is horrified by the surroundings and the company she has kept. She arrives home to find that Lheureux is demanding payment of 8,000 francs within twenty-four hours under threat of seizure. He is unmoved by Emma's threats and insinuates that she has friends to help her.

NOTES AND GLOSSARY:

'nous ferons sauter ensemble les *monacos*': *(slang)* 'we'll make the money fly'

***turne, bazar, chicard, chicandard, Breda-Street*:** *(slang)* translated in the Penguin edition as 'digs, outfit, swell, slick, Breda Street'. The first two of these words are still in common use. The general point is that these words are very innocuous indeed and would not shock in the way Homais intends

Cujas et Barthole: a French jurist (1522–90) and an Italian jurist (1314–57). Homais loves to show off whatever he knows about a subject, however little. He is so full of himself that he is quite unaware of Léon's desire to get away from him

elle alla le soir au bal masqué: 'she went in the evening to a masked ball'. Flaubert places this ball in the novel to contrast with the ball at Vaubyessard. It brings home to Emma and to the reader how low she has sunk

---

Part III, Chapter 7

The next morning the bailiff makes an inventory of the contents of the Bovarys' house. Emma and Félicité install his assistant in the attic so that Charles will not know he is there. Emma goes round the banks in Rouen to ask for a loan, in vain. In their hotel room she hints to Léon that he should steal the money from his firm. He conveniently remembers a friend due back that night from whom he could borrow: he promises to bring Emma the money at three o'clock the next afternoon.

In the coach back to Yonville, Emma is distraught; Homais by contrast is very pleased with himself. He is taking home some special loaves of bread for his wife; he shouts instructions to the beggar, telling him that his ailment would soon clear up if only he would eat well.

The next morning notices appear in Yonville advertising the sale of Emma's effects. Emma goes for help to the solicitor, Maître Guillaumin. He lets her speak though he knows her story already since he is in league with Lheureux. He finally says he will give her money, but tries to grasp her round the waist. Emma exclaims that she is to be pitied, not to be bought, and walks out.

Emma reflects bitterly that when Charles finds out what has happened she is going to have to suffer his forgiveness; she will never forgive him for having known her.

Madame Tuvache and Madame Caron observe Emma making some kind of appeal to Binet. They are scandalised to see her take Binet's hand.

Emma takes refuge with Madame Rollet. As she lies on the bed recalling the past, she remembers that Léon has promised to come and she sends Madame Rollet to meet him. Emma waits impatiently. Madame Rollet comes back alone. Emma thinks of Rodolphe. Surely he will help her if she offers herself to him.

NOTES AND GLOSSARY:

le gardien de la saisie: 'the bailiff's man'. His job is to make sure that the owners do not remove their effects from the house

la _Esméralda_ de Steuben, avec la _Putiphar_ de Schopin: Steuben and Schopin were popular painters in the mid-nineteenth century. Steuben painted two versions of _Esméralda_, in 1839 and 1842. The paintings signify that Guillaumin is a conventional well-to-do bourgeois with safe artistic tastes

Part III, Chapter 8

Emma makes her familiar way through Rodolphe's splendid house to his room. She charms him into telling her he still loves her. But when she asks him to lend her 3,000 francs, he becomes cold and tells her he does not have them. Emma glances round at the luxury in which Rodolphe lives and pours out all her resentment against him. She leaves the house in a daze, suffering no longer because of the money but from a sense of love betrayed.

She goes to Homais's house, gets Justin to give her the key to the store-room and swallows arsenic straight from the bottle.

She returns home, writes and seals a letter and, refusing to answer
Charles's questions, retires to bed. Progressively symptoms appear: a taste
of ink in the mouth, vomiting. Charles's consternation turns to anguish
when he reads the letter. Emma speaks kindly to Charles and asks to see
Berthe, who is terrified by her mother's appearance. Dr Canivet prescribes
an emetic: Emma vomits blood. Then Dr Larivière arrives from Rouen, a
commanding figure of the old school, revered and feared by his pupils. He
urges Charles to be brave and leaves the house, followed by Canivet who is
equally reluctant to have Emma die on his hands.

Homais invites Larivière to lunch, and the whole village is set to
providing fare for the great man. Homais displays his medical erudition,
unaware that Larivière sees through him and is making fun of him.
Villagers crowd in to get a free diagnosis of their ailments.

Canivet and Homais return to Emma's room where Bournisien is giving
her the last rites. She asks for a mirror and Charles hopes for a reprieve.
Then she begins to gasp for breath while Bournisien prays ever more
fervently. From the street comes the voice of the blind beggar singing his
song about a young woman in love. Emma laughs despairingly and dies.

NOTES AND GLOSSARY:

'mon mari avait placé toute sa fortune chez un notaire': 'my husband
                put all his money into the hands of a lawyer'. Most of
                this speech of Emma's is pure invention, but Flaubert
                creates sympathy for her by emphasising Rodolphe's
                hard-heartedness. When Emma denounces him in the
                following speeches, her account of him and of their
                relationship rings true

Cet affreux goût d'encre: 'That dreadful inky taste'. Flaubert's account
                of Emma's symptoms is factually correct. Readers of
                his time were shocked by his clinical precision. Death
                scenes were a commonplace of nineteenth-century lit-
                erature and art, but tended towards melodrama and
                moralising: the characters were simple stereotypes of
                good and bad; if the dying person was bad, death was
                shown as a punishment; if good, he or she was sur-
                rounded by grieving family and friends. For an inter-
                pretation of this death scene, see Part 3 of this book

le *Misereatur* et l'*Indulgentiam*: prayers which form part of the last rites
                for the dying in the Roman Catholic Church

Part III, Chapter 9

Charles has to be dragged away from Emma's corpse. With difficulty,
Homais and Bournisien get him to think about funeral arrangements. They

are amazed that he wants to have her buried in her wedding dress within three coffins.

Bournisien and Homais are the principal mourners at the wake. Homais spends the night challenging Bournisien to defend the apparent inconsistencies of Christianity. Charles comes and goes, his eyes constantly returning to Emma. In the early morning his mother arrives, followed in the evening by a stream of mourners each of whom is bored but resolved to be the last to leave the house. The following night Homais and Bournisien resume their squabbling until eventually, together, they fall asleep. Charles stands once more beside Emma and ruminates on the happiness he has lost, but when he lifts her veil the sight of her makes him cry out with horror. Bournisien and Homais wake up in the morning and take a snack together, in high good humour.

NOTES AND GLOSSARY:

un mensonge qui pût cacher l'empoisonnement: 'a lie to conceal the poisoning'. Homais wants to conceal the fact that Emma poisoned herself, partly because suicide is regarded by the Catholic faith as a sin, and Emma will not be permitted a religious burial. Moreover, he does not want people to know that she got the arsenic from his storeroom

d'Holbach: Paul Thiry, Baron d'Holbach (1723–89), a philosopher who wrote many anti-religious works

l'Encyclopédie: The great Encyclopedia which appeared in numerous volumes (1751–80). Its contributors were highly sceptical of revealed religion

Lettres de quelques juifs portugais: Both this work *(Letters of some Portuguese Jews)* and *Raison du christianisme (Proof of Christianity)* are minor religious tracts

Part III, Chapter 10

Emma's father faints when he sees the funeral procession. He had not known how to interpret the confused letter he had received from Homais, and his feelings fluctuated between hope and fear as he rode posthaste to Yonville. At the funeral, Charles finds some consolation in a despairing rage; Hippolyte wears the artificial leg Emma had bought for him. The funeral procession winds its way through the smiling countryside. Charles has to be restrained from throwing himself into the grave. Emma's death is lamented by the assembled mourners: Lheureux is particularly affected. Emma's father rides off, assuring Charles that he will still send him a turkey every year. Charles's mother rejoices that she has once again become the most important woman in her son's life. Charles lies awake thinking of Emma. Léon and Rodolphe sleep. Justin kneels crying on the grave—Lestiboudois thinks he is stealing potatoes.

NOTES AND GLOSSARY:

'Je m'en vas la conduire jusqu'au bout': 'I'll go along with her to the end'. Common colloquial usage for 'Je m'en vais'. Monsieur Rouault's simple warm-hearted grief contrasts with the self-satisfaction of Madame Bovary senior. In this chapter Flaubert gives a last thumbnail sketch of a number of his characters by contrasting their reactions to Emma's death

---

Part III, Chapter 11

Charles carries on living in the house with Berthe. Bills flood in. He finds Rodolphe's letter of farewell which he chooses to regard as homage from a platonic admirer. He becomes extravagant; he and Berthe are increasingly impoverished and abandoned.

Homais, having failed to cure the beggar's blindness, wages a successful campaign to have him locked up. His ambitions grow. He writes a statistical account of Yonville, and designs a magnificent tombstone for Emma.

Though Charles constantly thinks of Emma, her image fades in his mind. He quarrels with his mother and worries about Berthe's health.

Homais's family flourishes, but he longs to be awarded a decoration.

Charles discovers Emma's store of letters from Léon and Rodolphe. He shuts himself up in his house and neglects his patients. One day he meets Rodolphe. 'Non, je ne vous en veux plus' (I don't bear a grudge against you any more), he says, 'C'est la faute de la fatalité' (Fate is to blame). Rodolphe finds this comic and a bit abject. The next day Berthe finds Charles dead on the garden bench.

Homais has just been awarded the Legion of Honour.

NOTES AND GLOSSARY:

cho-ca, revalentia: preparations made from chocolate and various flours. They were mistakenly believed to have medicinal properties. Homais marches with the times, even— or especially—when the times are marching in the wrong direction. This chapter is based on character contrast: Charles succumbs grotesquely to genuine grief; Homais rises to a worthless triumph

'Sta viator . . . amabilem conjugam calcas: *(Latin)* 'Stop awhile, passer-by; you are treading on an amiable wife'

Part 3

Commentary

Madame Bovary is the story of a woman who tries to live life the way she feels it ought to be. The novel explains why she wants to do this, paints a picture of the society in which she lives, and shows how she comes into conflict with it. In this portrayal of a heroine set against the background of her environment, Flaubert blends and refines two of the main traditions of French nineteenth-century literature: Romanticism and Realism.

Romanticism

For the French Romantic writers of the beginning of the nineteenth century, the individual was supreme, and intensity of feeling was the highest value. Therefore, although the Romantic hero appears in many different forms—in the gentle melancholy of Lamartine's poetry, in the autobiographical poems and prose of Musset, in the melodramas of Victor Hugo—there are certain recurring features in his experience. He is constantly in search of new depths of feeling. His moods swing between elation and depression, between vibrant communion with nature or a fellow human being, and a sense of purposelessness and *ennui*. He is fascinated by love, especially unhappy or lost love, because such experiences offer intensity of emotion. But time makes emotion fade, and the hero is condemned to seek new experience elsewhere. He fears that he will never be able to fill the void at the centre of his existence and half longs for death, the great mystery and supreme experience of human life.

René, the hero of Chateaubriand's novel of the same name (1805), is one of the early archetypes of this kind of figure. Here he is, for example, at one with nature, rejoicing in the storms of his own emotions:

> Arise in haste, longed-for tempests, which shall bear René off to the wide spaces of another life! So saying, I strode along, face aflame, the wind whistling in my hair, sensible of neither wind nor wintry cold, enchanted, tormented and as if possessed by the demon of my heart.

Possessed by this treasured demon, René wanders from country to country. Finally, cursed by the incestuous love of his sister, he seeks refuge in the grandiose wilderness of Louisiana.

René also demonstrates a relationship between the hero and society typical of Romantic literature. René's capacity for suffering sets him apart from others and ultimately proves that he is superior to them. Although Chateaubriand has one of the characters in the novel condemn René as an irresponsible dreamer, he makes sure that the sympathy of the reader lies with his hero. When once, briefly, René tries to enter society, he is soon repelled by its petty concerns which contrast with the profundity of his own emotions. In fact, the ordinary world of social obligations and constraints plays next to no part in the novel. Although society disapproves of René, it has no power over him. He simply withdraws from it and continues to live by his own values. This portrayal of the relationship between society and the individual is in strong contrast to the way it appears in the Realist tradition.

Realism

There have always been writers of poetry and prose who have tried to describe the world as it is. The Realism of the nineteenth century, however, is of a specific kind. It stems from the great collective effort of eighteenth-century writers and philosophers to annex a new field of experience for methodological observation: society itself. In the preface of 1842 to his immense series of novels, *La Comédie humaine*, Balzac portrays himself as a scientific observer whose task is to give a picture of French society from the 1790s to the 1840s. He groups his novels systematically into those dealing with private life, life in Paris, life in the provinces, and so on. He presents his characters not as unique individuals but as representatives of a particular class or sub-group of society at a particular time.

The prestige of science, and eventually of Balzac himself, led other novelists to push further in the same direction. In the 1850s there emerged a small group who called themselves Realists. Their aim was to represent banal, everyday life without transforming it in any way. Much more ambitious was Emile Zola. His series of novels, *Les Rougon-Macquart*, aims to reflect the social history of France between 1852 and 1870 within the compass of the story of a single wide-flung family.

In all these broadly Realist novels, society and the individual are interdependent. Part of the novelist's task is to explain how each influences the other, which is why the physical and social setting of the characters' lives is usually described in detail. In Zola's work, the individual is entirely determined by environment and heredity, at least in theory. Balzac is more nuanced. In his novel *Le Père Goriot*, for example, he concludes a long description of a boarding-house and its owner, Madame Vauquer, with the remark: 'To sum up, her whole person explains the boarding-house, just as the boarding-house implies her person.' Notice here that Madame Vauquer has shaped her environment, rather than the reverse. Indeed, the novel as a whole shows how a determined individual can make a mark on society, albeit not without cost to himself. The young student and central character, Rastignac, learns that he can achieve his ambitions, but only if he becomes as unscrupulous as everyone else. As in Chateaubriand's *René*, society is seen to be petty and mean, but here escape is not the hero's chosen route. The exceptional individual asserts himself by adopting society's values.

What then is the balance between the individual and society in *Madame Bovary*? We shall be able to understand Emma Bovary better if we look first at the community in which she lives.

Society in *Madame Bovary*

Flaubert's portrayal of society has links with both the Romantic and the Realist traditions. The setting is almost contemporaneous with the time the novel was written. Various indications—for example, references to the King in the official's speech at the agricultural show—prove that the main events of the novel take place in the latter part of the reign of Louis-Philippe in the early 1840s. No dates, however, are given for Emma's marriage or death. Flaubert makes no links between the personal and the historical. He is concerned with the texture of ordinary life in a rural province remote from the excitement of great events.

Flaubert lays great store by being precise in his observations. The country wedding and the agricultural show are, among other things, exact reproductions of life as it was in the Normandy of the 1840s. Even the tiniest details are true to life. Coming home from Rouen one day, Homais buys 'cheminots' for his wife. Flaubert takes time to describe exactly what these are: a special kind of bread found only in that part of France. The same care goes into the description of less time-bound matters. Perhaps few readers will want to follow Flaubert into the full details of Emma's financial difficulties, but the essential point is that by a series of insidious, almost imperceptible steps she falls into the clutches of Lheureux. On the other hand, few who have read the book will ever forget the clinical accuracy with which Flaubert describes the agony of death by arsenic poisoning, or the miseries which follow the unsuccessful operation on Hippolyte's club-foot.

But none of this detail is described for its own sake. Flaubert transforms reality to make it serve his artistic purpose. This is what distinguishes him from the self-styled Realists of the 1850s, and explains why he once wrote that he had conceived this novel in hatred of Realism.

Flaubert arranges, simplifies and exaggerates. His apparently ordinary provincials become extraordinary because they are seen in the spotlight of Flaubert's satire. The people of Yonville are backward and ignorant. They regard Paris with a mixture of awe, envy and disapproval. Their ideas and arguments are second-hand, based on out-dated models. Their language, too, is second-hand, dominated by all kinds of clichés: romantic, religious, scientific and political. They have absolute confidence in their own values—self-interest, the security of routine, and pleasure (provided it poses no threat to social respectability)—and can conceive of no others. Their ambitions are limited to making money, gaining social prestige or achieving the modest happiness of reproducing themselves in their children. These characteristics are differently emphasised in different characters.

Major characters

Homais

As pharmacist, shopkeeper, journalist, writer of learned monographs on local topics, model husband and father, Homais is a splendid satirical portrait. He is loquacious, opinionated and, above all, self-important. He has his name blazoned over the chemist's shop in large letters. When reflecting on the occasional abstractedness of learned men, it comes naturally to him to think of them in ascending order as 'lawyer, doctor and chemist'. Intellectually, he is a believer in social and scientific progress. His speeches—he makes speeches rather than conversation—are full of pseudo-scientific words and half-baked information. Sometimes Flaubert makes fun of him in such a broad way that he becomes a figure of farce: few chemists could make a mistake as he does, even briefly, about the chemical formula for ammonia.

But there is a more sinister side to the presentation of this character. He is ruthlessly ambitious to achieve social recognition—which he eventually does with the award of the Legion of Honour. This, Flaubert seems to be saying, is the kind of person who rises to the top in contemporary society, at the expense of others, like the good-hearted Charles, or like the blind beggar who cannot be fitted into the myth of a society blessed by universal progress.

Léon

Emma's admirer and later her lover. Flaubert sketches his development from timid youth to the beginning of his bourgeois maturity.

As a solicitor's clerk in provincial Yonville, Léon has good reason to be bored but, having read Romantic literature, he dramatises himself in the role of Romantic hero. His first conversation with Emma is a parody of Romantic themes: the futility of life, the restless search for the infinite, the grandeur of feelings evoked by music and by nature. Is it really conceivable that a pianist would move his piano to a picturesque site in order to be inspired by nature?

In Paris Léon acquires a superficial sophistication which gives him the courage to bundle Emma into a cab. (Neither of them is now so naive as to believe the Romantic cliché that instinct had guided him to her hotel.) Léon is flattered by having a mistress. Soon, however, Emma's demands and her recklessness alarm him. Bourgeois caution asserts itself. He follows the advice of his mother and his employer to break with Emma: she could damage his career. And it would be unsafe to lend her money. Although this is a satirical portrait of bourgeois smallmindedness, we may also feel a touch of wry sympathy for Léon's dilemma: Emma is absorbing his personality, and he cannot cope with the situation in which he finds himself.

Charles

Emma's husband and the most complex character in the novel after Emma herself. He is presented primarily as a buffoon, a natural victim. In the first scene he brings disaster on himself by losing his cap. Later, he encourages Emma to go riding with Rodolphe and, later still, to stay on in Rouen without him and go to the opera with Léon. He suspects nothing. His former schoolmate remarks, 'Il serait maintenant impossible à aucun de nous de se rien rappeler de lui' (It would be impossible for any of us to remember the least thing about him now), but, on the contrary, Flaubert exaggerates his dullness so much that he becomes extremely memorable. For example, he is quite unable to follow the story of the opera and explains that this is because of the music which detracts from the words. Unexciting and unimaginative, he is on the face of it designed to be the opposite of all that Emma wants. The contrast is well brought out in their parallel reveries (Part II, Chapter 12). Charles dreams of a future which is just like the present, in which Berthe grows up to marry a man just like himself. She will be as happy as Charles imagines Emma to be. Meanwhile Emma is dreaming of life far away from Charles, and of the exotic places she will visit in company with Rodolphe, her ideal lover.

The reader may well be touched by Charles's naivety. His incompetence as a doctor, too, though ludicrous in the case of the club-foot operation, has overtones of tragedy when he fails to diagnose or treat Emma for arsenical poisoning. Charles's fate is tragic because he is genuinely, passionately devoted to his wife. The romantic yearnings of his youth, including the melancholy which made his expression 'presque intéressante' (almost interesting), have all focussed on her. His grief is genuine, even if its expression, influenced by Emma, takes a ridiculously exaggerated form: how she would have enjoyed the idea of being buried ' . . . dans sa robe de noces, avec des souliers blancs, une couronne. On lui étalera ses cheveux sur les épaules; trois cercueils, un de chêne, un d'acajou, un de plomb' (. . . in her wedding dress, with white shoes and a wreath, and her hair spread out over her shoulders. Three coffins, one oak, one mahogany, and one lead). It is a typical Flaubertian irony that Emma is blind to Charles's passion and does not live to see its full flowering.

Secondary characters

Madame Bovary senior

Charles's mother. A domineering woman and the dominant influence on him until he meets Emma. Since she is cautious, economical and unimaginative, the antithesis of Emma, the two women inevitably come into conflict. When Emma dies, she is happy to regain temporarily her supremacy over Charles. An unsympathetic character. (The main chapters in which she appears are Part I, Chapters 1, 4 and 7; Part II, Chapters 7 and 10; Part III, Chapters 2, 5 and 11.)

Charles-Denis-Bartholomé Bovary

Charles's father. An assistant surgeon (little more than a medical orderly) who retired from the army, married relatively well, and lived on his wife's income. He has an eye for the ladies and dazzles the provincials with his military charm. His wife fears he will make an impression on Emma who, however, is quite unmoved by his death. There was no need for Charles to try to soften the blow by asking Homais to break the news to her gently. It is another illustration of the gulf between Charles and Emma. (See Part I, Chapters 1 and 4; Part II, Chapter 3; Part III, Chapter 2.)

Héloïse Bovary

Charles's first wife. A forty-five-year-old widow who turns out not to be as rich as Charles's mother had thought when she encouraged Charles to marry her. She is jealous and possessive and helps us understand why Charles is attracted to Emma. (See Part I, Chapters 1 and 2.)

Monsieur Rouault

Emma's father. A wily peasant farmer who reckons Charles is a buffoon but not a bad match for his daughter. He is generous and sentimental, deeply attached to the memory of his dead wife. His account of how he grieved at her death suggests that Emma may have inherited some of the extravagance of her feelings from him. His letter to Emma and Charles (Part II, Chapter 10) is a model of simple, clumsy affection. A comic character but treated with some sympathy. (See Part I, Chapters 2, 3 and 4; Part II, Chapter 10; Part III, Chapter 10.)

Monsieur Binet

The local tax-collector at Yonville and captain of the fire brigade. He is a man of few words and regular habits: he dines every night at exactly the same time at the *Lion d'or* and has an obsessive hobby of making napkin rings. When he can get away with it, he is not above breaking the law, for example on duck-shooting. He is shocked when Emma asks him for money, possibly offering herself in return. A picture of the typical bourgeois who never lifts his eyes beyond the banal routine of his own preoccupations. (See Part II, Chapters 1, 8 and 10; Part III, Chapter 7.)

Bournisien

The parish priest of Yonville. A gentle giant, strong and dull-witted who does his duty according to his lights, but has no conception of spiritual needs beyond his routine tasks of teaching the catechism, urging sinners to repent and breaking the evil spell on sick cows. In defending the Church against Homais, Bournisien resorts to the clichés of authority or finds himself forced into comic paradox: when they are discussing the evils of the theatre and Homais objects that there are some saucy bits in the Bible, Bournisien replies that it's the Protestants, not the Catholics, who encourage their people to read the Bible. A good example of Flaubert's ability to caricature whilst being fair to a character at the same time. (See Part II, Chapters 1, 6, 11 and 14; Part III, Chapters 8 and 9.)

Rodolphe Boulanger

A local landowner and Emma's first lover, whom Flaubert presents unambiguously as a villain. He is an experienced and cynical womaniser: his first thoughts on seeing Emma are that it would be nice to have her, but how would he get rid of her afterwards? He seduces Emma at the agricultural show by manipulating the clichés of romantic love: he is alone and friendless; the two of them were meant for each other; true love is the most important thing in the world, far more important than society's rules and regulations. In fact, he does not believe any of this. His letter of farewell is a masterpiece of hypocrisy, which Flaubert makes clear by describing Rodolphe's thoughts as he composes it. (See Part II, Chapters 7, 8, 9, 10, 12 and 13; Part III, Chapter 8.)

Lheureux

A draper and seller of fancy goods who flatters and cajoles Emma into buying what she cannot afford. He makes money by lending her more money and charging interest on what he has lent. Then, when she can no longer pay, he sends in a bailiff to seize her effects. Flaubert makes clear that Lheureux habitually makes money in this way: his victim before Emma was Tellier of the *Café Français*. By the end of the novel he is beginning to threaten Madame Lefrançois of the *Lion d'or* by setting up a coach service which would call at his inn, not hers. Lheureux, like Homais, seems to be the kind of person who thrives in the society of the time. (See Part II, Chapters 1, 5, 8, 12 and 14; Part III, Chapters 2, 5, 6 and 10.)

Justin

Homais's apprentice, an orphan and distant relative of the Homais family. He conceives an adolescent passion for Emma Bovary. Flaubert gives a delicate portrayal of his awakening sensuality. Like Charles, he is heart-broken by her death — all the more so since she used him to get access to the arsenic — and he understands even less what has led her to suicide. Justin's perspective adds pathos to Emma's death. (See Part II, Chapters 3, 4, 7 and 14; Part III, Chapters 2, 8 and 10.)

Emma as a Romantic heroine

Flaubert's presentation of society conforms to a pattern which can be found in both Romantic and Realist literature. He finds its members petty and mean. He makes fun of his characters, sometimes with bitter irony, and holds their values up to ridicule. His attitude to Emma, however, is much more ambivalent.

Emma's private world is that of a Romantic heroine. Her life is a series of cycles which correspond to her states of feeling: from *ennui*, to expectation, to relative emotional fulfilment; then to disappointment and back to *ennui* again. These cycles structure the novel by providing a recurring framework for the main events: her marriage to Charles, her discovery of love with Léon, her passionate affair with Rodolphe, and her reckless liaison with Léon. Of course, each cycle is different from the one before. Flaubert comments that at the time of Charles's first appearance at her father's farm Emma regarded herself as utterly disillusioned 'with nothing more to learn and nothing more to feel'. Here Emma is adopting a Romantic pose modelled on René, acting weary of the world before she has experienced it. As the novel proceeds she experiences much more, thus each successive cycle encompasses a greater range of feeling: the heights are higher and the depths lower. The thrill of marriage lies all in the expectation. With Léon, Emma suffers the pangs of awakening and then frustrated love. Rodolphe arouses her sensuality and his departure reduces her to despair. She dominates Léon the second time round by the frenzy of her sensual and emotional demands.

But though she aspires to be a Romantic heroine, Emma is not a second René. In Part I, Chapter 6, Flaubert describes the books which Emma reads in her youth and the impression they leave on her. Although she reads the great Romantics, including Chateaubriand and Lamartine, her main fodder is second-rate, sub-romantic literature: romanticised history and historical romances.

Ce n'étaient qu'amours, amants, amantes, dames persécutées s'évanouissant dans des pavillons solitaires, postillons qu'on tue à tous les relais, chevaux qu'on crève à toutes les pages, forêts sombres, troubles du cœur, serments, sanglots, larmes et baisers, nacelles au clair de lune, rossignols dans les bosquets, *messieurs* braves comme des lions, doux comme des agneaux, vertueux comme on ne l'est pas, toujours bien mis, et qui pleurent comme des urnes.

(They were all about love and lovers, damsels in distress swooning in lonely lodges, postillions slaughtered along the road, horses ridden to death on every page, gloomy forests, troubles of the heart, vows, sobs, tears, kisses, rowing-boats in the moonlight, nightingales in the grove, gentlemen brave as lions and gentle as lambs, too virtuous to be true, invariably well dressed, and weeping like fountains.)

Chateaubriand presents René as an exceptional, original being; Emma is exceptional only in the persistence with which she tries to make life conform to her ideal. And unlike René, she is set within the framework of society — the most banal and ordinary of societies, a small town in the provinces.

This is why her behaviour seems so incongruous. Sometimes the effect is amusing, for example, when she expresses the wish to have been married at midnight by candlelight, or startles Rodolphe by enquiring whether he has got his pistols ready (as if he would need or want pistols to deal with Charles!). It is this persistent search for drama which leads to her downfall. Although Rodolphe is transparently a villain, she allows herself to be taken in by him because he is saying what she wants to hear. Even as she dies, she still in part acts the role of the tragic Romantic heroine cursed by fate: she takes leave of life with what is indicated to be an elegant suicide note, summons her usually neglected child for a sentimental farewell and kisses the cross with sensual, theatrical passion. Unfortunately, reality refuses to be stage-managed like the last act of a Romantic opera. Flaubert points this out by the use of precise, clinical description of the true effects of the poison. Arsenic induces terrible sickness, so Berthe is not touched by grief but is terrified when she sees her mother's suffering. Meanwhile Emma is not even the main focus of attention. The other characters go about their trivial everyday affairs, eating, drinking, trying to impress, and using the doctor to have their own petty ailments diagnosed. The incongruity between life as it is and life as Emma imagines it has now become gruesome and horrifying.

All this has made some critics take the view that, in Emma, Flaubert is portraying Romanticism as a disease, showing the disastrous effects it can have on a certain kind of temperament. Perhaps if Emma had been educated differently she could have grown up to be a normal, well-adjusted member of society. An extreme version of this view is represented within the novel by Charles's mother. She argues that Emma will improve only if Charles cuts off her supply of novels. Yet would any reader of the novel really wish to see Emma become well adjusted to the society of Yonville — to become more like her mother-in-law, for example? This is where the portrayal of the other characters becomes important. Emma may seem foolish, naive, misguided, thoughtless, even cruel at times; but these defects appear very slight when compared with those of the other characters, like the petty jealousy of Charles's mother or the monstrous egoism of Homais. The scenes which precede Emma's suicide drive home this contrast. Guillaumin tries to buy her; Léon does not have the courage to say he will not help her; Rodolphe callously and blatantly lies by saying he does not have the money. The reader's sympathy goes out to Emma, especially when Flaubert makes it clear that what hurts Emma most is the realisation that Rodolphe does not and did not love her: 'Elle ne souffrait que de son amour et sentait son âme l'abandonner par ce souvenir' (Only in her love did she suffer; just at the thought of the memory she felt her soul escape from her). This pinpoints a basic difference between Emma and the majority of those among whom she lives. Their values are essentially selfish, material and limited to the world they see around them. Emma aspires, however imperfectly, to a different and better world, an ideal world in which people will live by values of love and loyalty. Flaubert once wrote that, 'une âme se mesure à la dimension de son désir' (the measure of a soul is the magnitude of its aspirations). By this yardstick Emma is undoubtedly superior to the society in which she lives.

There are other critics who think that, in Flaubert's eyes, Emma's underlying defect is not her Romantic imagination but rather that she tries to turn her dreams into reality. She is not just a dreamer but a woman of action — at least within the narrow limits that her social status allows. First dominated by Rodolphe, she then dominates Léon and makes him play the role of the passionate lover. The more she is frustrated in attaining the ideal, the more she seeks compensation in the material world. She revels in the luxury which Lheureux provides for her. She pushes Charles into the club-foot operation to gain social prestige. At the end, she still has time to glance round Guillaumin's room and think, 'Voilà une salle à manger . . . comme il m'en faudrait une' (This is the kind of dining room I could do with). To some extent, then, Emma shares the values of her society. By engaging with the world, she reduces herself to its level. A better response, Flaubert implies, would be to turn one's back on the world. This, of course, is precisely what René did by fleeing to the wilderness of Louisiana. If you accept this interpretation of Emma, then you see Flaubert as a Romantic, in direct line of descent from Chateaubriand.

Impersonality

It is hard to tell to what extent the reader is meant to sympathise with Emma. Flaubert intended this to be so. A comparison with Balzac can illuminate the point. In Balzac's novels the reader is always aware of the author's personality. Balzac writes as if he were talking to you, telling you about story, characters and what you are to think of them. Here is a striking example of his personal tone from the beginning of *Le Père Goriot*:

> When you have read of the secret sorrows of Old Goriot you will dine with unimpaired appetite, blaming the author for your callousness, taxing him with exaggeration, accusing him of having given wings to his imagination. But you may be certain that this drama is neither fiction nor romance. All is true, so true that everyone can recognise the elements of the tragedy in his own household, in his own heart perhaps.

Although Flaubert also comments on his characters from time to time, he does not talk to his readers like this. He thought that the personal views of the author ought not to be apparent in a novel. He once wrote that 'the novelist has no right to express his opinion on anything'; and on another occasion: 'I believe that great art is scientific and impersonal'. These remarks, made in letters to George Sand when he was writing *L'Education sentimentale*, are no less relevant to *Madame Bovary*. Of course they do not mean that Flaubert has no opinions. We have already seen how strongly these come across in his presentation of the people of Yonville. How then does he express them? Another letter to George Sand gives the clue: 'The best thing to do is quite simply to portray the things which exasperate you. Dissection is a form of vengeance.' Flaubert conveys his opinions implicitly, by the way he tells his story, by the order of events and by his choice of words. We shall now look at some of the techniques which he invented or perfected.

Juxtaposition

Flaubert plays his characters off against one another. Emma contrasts with Charles: he is slow and dull, contented with what he has; she is lively, bored and dissatisfied. Homais, the believer in progress, is set against Bournisien, the upholder of traditional faith. Emma's two lovers are contrasted in experience, motivation and social class. This same technique of juxtaposition structures many of the chapters in the novel. The subject lends itself to contrasts. Dream and reality are constantly at odds, as for example during the opera. Emma imagines herself wandering the earth with the tenor, Lagardy; in fact, she is stuck in a stuffy, smoke-filled theatre with a man who cannot even follow the plot. But Flaubert's delight in juxtaposition carries him further than the subject demands. The visit to the château La Vaubyessard is based on an elaborate series of contrasts between the life of the aristocracy and Emma's own home life. The interview between Emma and Bournisien shows them living in quite different worlds. Most striking of all are the juxtapositions in the chapter on the agricultural show.

This chapter (Part II, Chapter 8) is constructed of layer upon layer of parallels and contrasts. First, Emma and Rodolphe are set against the rest of the town. For both groups it is a time of expectation which will lead through a series of ritual moves to a longed-for climax. That ritual is largely composed of speeches: the romantic rhetoric of Rodolphe's declaration of love contrasts with the political rhetoric of Monsieur Lieuvain's speech. Although the topics are different, the speeches are equally cliché-ridden and insincere. The villagers are as entranced by Monsieur Lieuvain as Emma is captivated by Rodolphe. Here lies another contrast: Rodolphe manipulates Romantic clichés; Emma naively accepts them at face value.

The effect of these juxtapositions is to create irony which cuts both ways. Emma and Rodolphe are as grotesque as the townspeople. Those who make the speeches are no more or less condemned than those who are foolish enough to be taken in by them. This double irony is very typical of Flaubert in *Madame Bovary*. Sometimes, however, the commentary is more one-sided, and the critical spotlight turned in a particular direction. Catherine Leroux, the simple peasant woman, stands out in contrast to the bourgeois worthies and dignitaries. In giving her a medal for fifty-four years of service, they are patronising her and patting themselves on the back for their own fairness and generosity—just as they have exploited her for the last half-century. Their behaviour is all the more effectively condemned in that Flaubert does not glamorise Catherine but presents her in the truth of her limitations, as a dumb beast with the trappings of a superstitious faith. On the other hand, a few pages later Flaubert uses one of these same bourgeois, Monsieur Derozerays, the chief presenter of prizes, to comment on the climax to Rodolphe's speech:

> Et il saisit sa main; elle ne la retira pas.
> 'Ensemble de bonnes cultures!' cria le président.
> —Tantôt, par exemple, quand je suis venu chez vous . . .
> 'A M. Bizet, de Quincampoix.'
> —Savais-je que je vous accompagnerais?
> 'Soixante et dix francs!'

—Cent fois même, j'ai voulu partir, et je vous ai suivie, je suis resté.
'Fumiers.'

(He took her hand, and she did not withdraw it.
'General Prize!' cried the Chairman.
'Just now, for instance, when I came to call on you . . . '
'Monsieur Bizet of Quincampoix.'
' . . . how could I know that I should escort you here?'
'Seventy francs!'
'And I've stayed with you, because I couldn't tear myself away,
though I've tried a hundred times.'
'Manure!')

(Part II, Chapter 8)

The prize-giving has come for Rodolphe, just as it has for the farmers: they
get their prizes in cash, he gets Emma. There is not a word of truth in what
he says about Emma's effect on him since his campaign has been very
precisely mapped out in advance. What could be more appropriate than
Flaubert's indirect comment: 'Manure', or, more colloquially, 'What a
load of muck'?

Point of view

Who tells the story of *Madame Bovary*? For the most part it is a nameless
narrator who knows all about everything. Not merely does he describe
what happens and where it happens, he also tells us about the history of the
characters, and he takes us inside them to describe their thoughts. Yet even
though Flaubert writes in the tradition of omniscient narration which he
shares with most nineteenth-century French novelists, he repeatedly shows
events from the point of view of particular characters. There is a broad
overall pattern to these shifts. Flaubert approaches his subject from the
outside. Part I, Chapter 1 begins as if told by a former classmate of Charles.
Then, until just before the end of Part I, Chapter 5, we are given Charles's
perspective on events. Thereafter, for the bulk of the novel, Emma's view
predominates. After her death, the narrative voice becomes increasingly
distant from the characters. It summarises events which take place over a
lengthy period of time; one might describe it as taking a bird's eye view.

This general pattern, however, is only a rough guide to what happens in
the novel. In fact, the point of view is constantly shifting, from character
to character, from close-up to distant. The effects vary but are often
dramatic. For example, when Emma and Léon begin their whirlwind tour
round Rouen in a taxicab, Flaubert draws a discreet blind over the scene,
literally and metaphorically. The point of view switches suddenly from
Emma and Léon to the minds of the good bourgeois of Rouen who catch

glimpses of this cab hurtling round their town. They cannot fathom what is going on. Here Flaubert is making fun of naive provincials. Another shift makes such characters appear in a more threatening light. When Emma appeals to Binet for money, the scene is witnessed by Madame Tuvache and Madame Caron who dash upstairs to get a good view. 'On devrait fouetter ces femmes-là!'(Women like that should be whipped!) says Madame Tuvache. By adopting the viewpoint of these respectable women Flaubert satirises their petty lust for gossip as well as their protestations of outraged morality.

Adoption of a particular point of view often, though not always, gives a peculiar character to Flaubert's descriptions of people and places. They tell us as much about the observer as about whatever is observed. For example, in the course of the novel Emma's eyes are described at various times as being brown, blue or black. It has been claimed that this is a mistake on Flaubert's part. On the other hand, it can be considered a good if extreme illustration of the fact that different people see her in different ways at different times. Both Léon and Rodolphe see her eyes as black. Theirs is a simple and, in Rodolphe's case, a crude view based on the stereotype of the attractive woman. Rodolphe does not so much describe Emma as make a mental list of her good points: 'De belles dents, les yeux noirs, le pied coquet, et de la tournure comme une Parisienne!' (pretty teeth, dark eyes, trim little foot, turned out like a Parisian!). This is a string of clichés, the points which make Emma an attractive potential mistress. Charles, on the other hand, observes Emma closely. The first time he notices her eyes they seem to him to be brown shaded to black by her eyelashes. Newly married, he studies them again at leisure:

> Vus de si près, ses yeux lui paraissaient agrandis, surtout quand elle ouvrait plusieurs fois de suite ses paupières en s'éveillant; noirs à l'ombre et bleu foncé au grand jour, ils avaient comme des couches de couleurs successives, et qui, plus épaisses dans le fond, allaient en s'éclaircissant vers la surface de l'émail.

> (Seen so close, her eyes appeared enlarged, especially when she blinked them open several times in succession on waking. Black in the shadow, and a rich blue in broad daylight, they seemed to hold successive layers of colour, darkest at the depths and glowing brighter towards the surface.)

(Part I, Chapter 5)

What *was* the colour of Emma's eyes? There is no correct answer to that question. But it is clear that to Charles, her adoring husband, she was all women rolled into one. The 'real' colour of her eyes is much less important than the fascination they exercise on him and the pleasure he takes in describing them.

Free indirect speech

She wondered what made her life so miserable?

What made her life so miserable?

The first of the above sentences tells us what the character thought; it is an example of indirect speech. The second sentence hints that this is what a character thought, but does not say so explicitly; this is known grammatically as free indirect speech. Flaubert uses a great deal of free indirect speech in *Madame Bovary*. Here is an example.

N'importe! elle n'était pas heureuse, ne l'avait jamais été. D'où venait donc cette insuffisance de la vie, cette pourriture instantanée des choses où elle s'appuyait? . . . Mais, s'il y avait quelque part un être fort et beau, une nature valeureuse, pleine à la fois d'exaltation et de raffinements, un coeur de poète sous une forme d'ange, lyre aux cordes d'airain, sonnant vers le ciel des épithalames élégiaques, pourquoi, par hasard, ne le trouverait-elle pas?

(No matter, she still wasn't happy, she never had been. What caused this inadequacy in her life? Why did everything she leaned on instantaneously decay? . . . Oh, if somewhere there were a being strong and handsome, a valiant heart, passionate and sensitive at once, a poet's spirit in an angel's form, a lyre with strings of steel, sounding elegiac epithalamiums to the heavens, then why should she not find that being?)

(Part III, Chapter 6)

Free indirect speech, as it is used here, allows Flaubert to overcome the limitations of realism. Emma could never speak like this. Flaubert is distilling her thoughts and expressing them in a way which gives them maximum force. An epithalamium is a song or poem celebrating a marriage; an elegy is a mournful, plaintive poem, especially a lament for a dead. Could Emma have known either word? Yet, combined in the image of a lyre sounding its song to heaven, these two words give effective expression to Emma's Romantic longing for experience which will be sensual, mystical and melancholy. Similarly, the structure and rhythm of the sentences heighten their meaning. The third sentence is a striking example of Flaubert's use of triplets. It begins with an abrupt change of mood in the single syllable, 'Mais . . . '. Then follow three parallel phrases, each of which is elaborated and expanded to become longer than the previous one: 'un être fort et beau, une nature valeureuse . . . un coeur de poète . . .' . Another, much briefer set of three phrases concludes the sentence: 'pourquoi, par hasard, ne le trouverait-elle pas?' Again, each phrase is longer than the one before. The whole sentence conveys the swings in Emma's moods. The crescendo of her aspirations in the first part of the sentence collapses into the modest, almost despairing plea of the final triplet.

In addition, this use of free indirect speech is an aspect of Flaubert's manipulation of point of view. In the passage quoted above, Flaubert is close to Emma yet at a distance from her, conveying her thoughts yet not speaking with her voice. This ambiguity encourages the reader to see irony in the passage: perhaps there is a difference between what is said and what we are meant to understand. A particularly good example of this ironical gap appears in Emma's reflections after the failure of the club-foot operation. How could she ever have believed that Charles could succeed? 'Comment donc avait-elle fait (elle qui était si intelligente) pour se méprendre encore une fois?' (How could she have deceived herself again, she who was so intelligent?). But is Emma Bovary so intelligent? The use of free indirect speech makes us question the point. Is she intelligent at all, or is this part of her Romantic inheritance: a quite mistaken belief that in this, as in other things, she is a superior being? A similar effect can be found in the passage quoted at the beginning of this section. The images of the first triplet are successively more grandiose. They culminate in the elegaic epithalamium, the funereal wedding song. Although this image expresses Emma's aspirations, it also makes fun of them in that it is an incongruous, even a grotesque juxtaposition of ideas. As so often in the novel, the reader does not know whether to weep for Emma or to laugh at her.

Emma Bovary and Flaubert

Flaubert may or may not have made the famous remark which is often attributed to him: 'Emma Bovary, c'est moi'. But he certainly did once write that 'ce coeur que j'étudiais était le mien' (the heart that I was studying was my own). Emma is in part a portrait of himself. She belongs to the same generation as Flaubert. The literature which she reads reflects what Flaubert himself had read as a child and young man. Her Romantic enthusiasm and extravagance, her taste for the exotic, her search for an all-consuming passion, all echo the mood of Flaubert's early works. Her bitter disillusionment and disappointment, her scorn for the mediocrity of bourgeois life and values are constant themes of Flaubert's correspondence. Even some of the overt differences between Flaubert and Emma turn out to conceal parallels. Emma is a woman; she comes from a lower social class than Flaubert; she reads without discrimination. These differences make her more powerless than Flaubert to establish and live by her own values; but they reflect his own sense of impotence in the face of the dominant values of society, which, in the novel, are embodied in Homais.

There is, however, one key difference between Flaubert and Emma.

'Elle rejetait comme inutile tout ce qui ne contribuait pas à la consomma-tion immédiate de son coeur—étant de tempérament plus sentimentale qu'artiste' (she rejected as useless whatever did not administer to her heart's immediate fulfilment—being of a sentimental rather than an artistic temperament) (Part I, Chapter 6). Emma's prime limitation is that she cannot withdraw from life but continues to seek fulfilment within it. For Flaubert, on the other hand, temperament and ability make it partially possible to escape the real world and construct a parallel one in which the real world is transformed and denounced. In other words Flaubert seeks, and finds, fulfilment in art. His creed, he explained to Louise Colet, was 'l'acceptation ironique de l'existence et sa refonte plastique et complète par l'art' (the ironic acceptance of existence and its complete remelting and remoulding by art).

Emma Bovary is a distorted projection of Flaubert's image of himself. She is partly what he might have been, partly what he had been, partly a caricature, exaggerated beyond anything he could ever have been. This ultimately explains the ambivalence of his attitude towards her—that delightful ambivalence which gives readers scope for their own interpretations and projections.

Part 4

Hints for study

Structure

As you read *Madame Bovary* try to keep in mind the outline of the story.
Individual chapters make more sense when fitted into an overall
framework. Flaubert divided the novel into three parts. Part I introduces
Charles and Emma; Part II deals with Léon and Rodolphe; Part III returns
to Léon and shows Emma's downfall and its aftermath. This structure
raises a number of questions. Flaubert was concerned that readers might
find the beginning of the novel too slow; yet he felt it was essential to
establish his characters, to show what they were like and the context in
which they lived, before showing them in action. Why does he begin with
Charles rather than Emma? (And what is the point of giving Charles
another wife first?) Where do you think the action begins? Is it possible to
pinpoint a specific chapter, or is it rather a case of gradual acceleration, or
even of bursts of activity interspersed with periods of inaction?

Another way to think about the structure of the novel is to consider it in
terms of the development of Emma's personality. Read Part I, Chapter 6
and make a note of some of the main features of her personality as it is
described there. Now ask yourself some questions about Emma in the
novel as a whole. Does she change or does she stay the same? If she does
change, what are the main changes? (Are there some ways in which she
stays the same?) Flaubert originally intended that Emma would have an
affair with Léon followed by an affair with Rodolphe. What did he gain by
splitting her relationship with Léon into two parts, the first part before her
liaison with Rodolphe and the second part afterwards? What changes have
taken place in Emma—and in Léon—between these two experiences? To
help answer some of these questions you could, for example, read and
compare Part II, Chapter 2 with Part II, Chapter 15 and Part III, Chapter 1.

Tone

Tone is the expression of attitude which accompanies speech. A speaker's
or writer's tone may be warm or cold, indifferent or enthusiastic, scornful
or admiring, sincere or ironical. Tone is usually easy to grasp when one
can see and hear a speaker, even when he or she is using irony and means
the opposite of what is said: 'Thank you for coming' may quite clearly not

be an expression of gratitude if you have arrived for a class twenty minutes late. But one cannot see or hear a novelist. He or she relies on words alone to convey meaning. Catching the tone can sometimes be particularly tricky with Flaubert since, as we have seen, he preferred to refrain from commenting on characters and situation; and his tone varies widely from lyrical warmth through playful humour to biting irony and satire. One helpful way to catch Flaubert's tone is to do what he himself often did when writing the novel, which was to read it aloud. You can do this on your own—if you don't mind being taken for an eccentric by anyone who happens to overhear—or, much better, with a group of friends, and then discuss your reactions. Here are some passages which lend themselves to a dramatic reading:

Part II, Chapter 2: Homais, Charles, Léon and Emma at the *Lion d'or*.

Part II, Chapter 6: Emma and Bournisien. How does Flaubert convey that these two characters are on entirely different wave-lengths? By what they say? By the kinds of language they use?

Part II, Chapter 8: the agricultural show. Read part of Monsieur Lieuvain's speech where it alternates with the conversation between Emma and Rodolphe, and the part where Monsieur Derozerays announces the prize-winners. What contrasts and similarities can you find in the themes and how they are expressed? What does Flaubert gain by splicing these speeches together? (Would it have made any difference if he had given the whole of Monsieur Lieuvain's speech first and then continued: 'Meanwhile, Emma and Rodolphe . . . '?)

Part II, Chapter 9: Emma and Rodolphe in the forest. Read from the point where they dismount from their horses to the description of Emma as evening falls. How does Emma feel about this experience and how does Rodolphe feel about it? Does Flaubert establish the contrast between their feelings by what they say or by how he describes the scene and their thoughts? The paragraph beginning 'Les ombres du soir descendaient . . . ' (the evening shadows began to fall . . .) is one of the few in the novel which show Emma content, emotionally fulfilled. What imagery does Flaubert use and how does he manipulate the sentence structure to achieve this effect of sensual fulfilment?

Part III, Chapter 1: Emma, Léon and the beadle in the cathedral at Rouen. The beadle is a figure of fun, but are Emma and Léon any less so? Flaubert sets the scene up like an incident in a farce: each character has one thought in mind and follows his own course of action regardless of the others. What does each character want and what is amusing about their interaction?

Critical commentary

A critical commentary is an exercise in textual analysis. It has its origins in a French exercise known as 'exposition de texte', but as practised in the English-speaking world its format is less strict. You may be asked to write a commentary in place of a term essay or an examination question. You can also use the technique of commentary writing for private study, to get the most out of a chapter or even a few paragraphs.

As you approach your chosen passage, there are two main questions to consider. What are its principal themes? How are these themes or ideas expressed? The first priority is to get a good idea of the context in which the passage is set, especially what comes before it. This helps establish by contrast what is important in the passage itself. Does it carry the story forward? Does it introduce a new character, or show a familiar one in a new light? Does it develop an existing theme or bring in a new one? Does it introduce a change of mood or pace, signalled perhaps by a change of narrative technique? Note down what strikes you most under the two headings 'Themes' and 'Means of Expression'. It may well be helpful to consider how the passage develops. Is it divided into sections or paragraphs? If so, what is new in each of these? To begin with, your observations will be somewhat haphazard and fragmented, but as you read and re-read the passage—taking care that you understand every word—you ought to begin to see relationships between themes and means of expression. Are there, for instance, any recurrent images in the passage? If so, how do they relate to the main themes?

The question of coherence becomes even more crucial when you start to think about organising the material for presentation. It is usually a mistake to go through the passage chronologically line by line or even paragraph by paragraph. The danger of this approach is that it is too easy to fall into re-telling the story: a commentary is not a summary. A much better way to present the material is to deal with different topics in different paragraphs. There are no absolute rules here but it makes sense to start with a broad overall view and then gradually work down to details. This may mean starting with some discussion of themes and then working through narrative techniques and finishing with matters of style. It is essential to relate everything to what you see as the main function or functions of the passage in the novel. For example, there is little point in saying simply that there is a metaphor in line 17, or that the third paragraph consists largely of short sentences. Although these are relevant initial observations, you should go further than merely noting them. What does that metaphor, or those short sentences, contribute to the themes or mood of the passage as a whole?

As an example, let us take Part II, Chapter 2 of *Madame Bovary*, which describes the arrival of Emma and Charles in Yonville. One of the first things you might notice about this chapter is its form. It begins and ends with a few descriptive paragraphs — the arrival at the inn, the arrival at the new house — but the bulk of the chapter is composed of dialogue. Part of its function in the novel is to introduce new characters by letting them speak for themselves. Another part of its function concerns Emma. Here the context gives the clue. Emma had married Charles with high expectations which have not been fulfilled in Tostes. So it is with a sense of expectation that she arrives in Yonville. Will Yonville be different?

Many indications in the passage suggest that it will not be. The very first paragraph re-establishes an already familiar contrast between Emma and Charles. Emma, eager to see her new surroundings, gets out of the coach first; Charles is so unaffected by the new experience that he has fallen asleep. Whatever else may be new in Yonville, Emma is still tied to Charles. Léon's boredom is another ominous hint for the future. There are no interesting walks, he assures Emma, and nothing to do: Yonville is isolated, provincial and dead. A number of Emma's initial experiences of her new environment confirm this gloomy picture. The service at the hotel is slow and slovenly: Flaubert draws out the sentence which describes Artémise, the waitress, to emphasise how the meal drags on. Moreover, the new home is cold and unwelcoming, with furniture piled higgledy-piggledy in the middle of the room.

Léon's denigration of Yonville contrasts with Homais's enthusiasm. For Homais, everything about Yonville is of passionate interest: weather, social conditions, religious beliefs, common illnesses, the doctor's house, and, most of all, himself. From Emma's point of view Homais adds to the negative image of Yonville. His contribution to the conversation is a monologue. He wanders inconsequentially from topic to topic. The paragraph beginning 'Du reste, disait l'apothicaire . . . ' (Moreover, said the apothecary . . .) is an exquisite analysis of the art of the bore. Flaubert constructs the second half of it as a single sentence, packed full of parentheses, gratuitous additions and subsidiary clauses; it is designed to stop anyone else from interrupting the speaker. From the reader's point of view, however, Homais's appearance adds colour to the novel. His prejudices, his pretentiousness, his self-importance add a new element of outrageous caricature. He uses long words, medical and scientific jargon, without knowing what he is talking about. Twenty-four degrees Centigrade is about seventy-three, not fifty-four Fahrenheit; ammonia contains not a whiff of oxygen. Although Emma may be set for a bad time in Yonville, the reader is clearly going to have some fun in the company of Homais.

Is there then no hope for Emma in Yonville? The nature of her conversation with Léon suggests that there is. They discover that they have many tastes in common: travel, nature, music and literature. But perhaps this apparent communion of souls is not quite as innocent as it seems. The third and fourth paragraphs of the chapter deal with the effect of Emma on Léon. With her dress lifted to reveal her ankles, her form illuminated by the glow of the fire, Emma is a picture of elegance and sensuality. In the conversation which follows, Léon's aim is partly to impress, to make himself seem interesting to this highly attractive young woman, to convince her that they do have much in common. So wherever she leads, he follows, even when she suddenly switches direction and declares that she has no sympathy with gentle melancholy poets, commonplace heroes and moderate feelings.

What Emma and Léon truly have in common is the old clichés of Romanticism. For Emma, sunset over the sea elevates the soul and gives intimations of the infinite. Léon caps this with another rather hackneyed image: the mountains. One can have no notion of how poetic the lakes, how full of charm the waterfalls, how gigantic the glaciers! To describe a glacier as gigantic is to do no more than state the obvious. The enthusiasm, the elevation of Léon's tone contrasts amusingly with the flatness of the images.

This brings us to a final feature of the chapter. Like so many others in *Madame Bovary*, it is based on the use of juxtapositions. The aspirations of Emma and Léon show up the blinkered views and interests of Homais. Yet even while we sympathise with them, and with Emma in particular, we are also being encouraged to laugh at them: Homais's pedestrian ramblings show up by contrast the extravagance of the young couple's unconvincing Romantic posing.

Essays and examination questions

If you are asked to write an essay about *Madame Bovary* during the term, you will have time to think about the title, to consult your teacher or tutor about it, and to re-read the novel with the subject of the essay in mind. In an examination you are on your own, you have to work at speed, and you will not usually have the text in front of you. These differences suggest how important it is to prepare for an examination. At the most elementary level you must have a good knowledge of the text. This does not necessarily mean that you should learn a string of quotations by heart. Although a brief quotation or two can help support a point, very often a reference to the novel will do instead. For instance, if in an examination essay you are discussing how Flaubert makes fun of Homais, you could refer to Homais's manner of speaking, his pseudo-scientific vocabulary, his inaccuracies. While you should give examples of each of these, you do not necessarily need to quote three or four consecutive lines from the text. In a term essay, on the other hand, you would certainly be expected to provide quotations. In fact, a useful technique of presentation consists in making a general point, then giving a quotation, and finally commenting with a couple of sentences on how precisely your quotation illustrates the general point.

A more useful kind of preparation for examinations is thinking about the text beforehand from a variety of points of view. Practice in doing this will help you to organise your thoughts at short notice in the examination. Here are some typical topics which you might find as essay or examination questions on *Madame Bovary*:

(a) At the end of *Madame Bovary*, Charles observes: 'C'est la faute de la fatalité'. Show to what extent, if at all, you would agree with this comment, applying it to both Charles and Emma.

(b) 'The central theme of *Madame Bovary* is the conflict between reality and a private dream-world.' Discuss this assertion, paying particular attention to the techniques and style which Flaubert has adopted in the novel.

(c) Examine the presentation of the characters of Homais, Lheureux and Bournisien in *Madame Bovary*, and show in what ways they contrast with Emma and Charles.

(d) 'L'art n'est pas fait pour peindre les exceptions' (Flaubert). To what extent has Flaubert been true to this precept in *Madame Bovary*?

(e) 'Flaubert is the great novelist of inaction, of boredom, of immobility.' Discuss this judgement.

(f) Who and what are the targets of Flaubert's satire in *Madame Bovary*? What means does he use to attack them?

(g) Discuss the presentation of organised religion and religious belief in *Madame Bovary*.

(h) 'In some respects, Charles and Emma are quite alike: each has an ideal and blinkered vision, each is used by the other characters, and above all, each is viewed by the author objectively and dispassionately.' How far would you agree with these statements about *Madame Bovary*?

(i) '*Madame Bovary* is a great comic novel.' Discuss.

To tackle questions like these successfully, you must do certain things. Firstly, make sure you understand the question. For instance, in example (a), what is the meaning of the word 'fatalité'? Fate, certainly, but what kind of fate? Something beyond human comprehension which strikes out of the blue, or something which is intelligible because one can see its origins in social and psychological factors? One might want to argue that Charles is talking about the first type of fate, whereas what Flaubert shows in *Madame Bovary* is the latter type.

Secondly, you must tackle every part of the question. In the essay about fate you are asked to apply Charles's comment to both Emma and Charles himself. If you only discuss Emma you make it very difficult for the examiner to give you anything more than half-marks for the question. It would be equally unwise to discuss Emma and Léon. The golden rule is to answer all that the question asks of you, and only that. You may find it useful to begin tackling a question by underlining all its key words, in this case: 'faute', 'fatalité', 'Emma' and 'Charles'. There is one other key phrase here: 'to what extent, if at all' do you agree with the judgement quoted? This is a typical examiner's ploy. It invites you in your turn to pass a cautious judgement. At some point in the essay you should answer this question explicitly. Your answer is likely to be a balanced one. 'To some extent this comment is justified because . . . but on the other hand . . . '

This brings us to a third point relevant to both term and examination essays. How should they be organised? Any essay must make a variety of points and each point must be supported by examples. Try your best to put your points in a logical order. Very often this will mean building up towards the most important point, the clinching argument. Put first the case with which you do not agree, then contest it with more powerful counter-arguments. A plan is essential. Do not be tempted to think that time spent on a plan in an examination is time wasted. On the contrary, you are all the more in need of a plan when shortage of time makes it vital to be both concise and comprehensive. An outline plan for the essay on fate might look like this:

Introduction:
The context in which Charles makes this statement (to Rodolphe after Emma's death); what he is referring to (Emma's affairs with Léon and Rodolphe; the whole sequence of events which led to her death; the wreck of his own life). Two ways of looking at the question: fate meaning something beyond human comprehension, fate meaning social or psychological determinism.

Fate as something beyond human understanding:
(1) The blind beggar. A sinister figure hinting that Emma is doomed to destruction. His appearances in the novel (as she leaves Léon in Rouen, at her death), his blindness (traditional characteristic of personifications of fate, suggesting its indiscriminate, inexplicable nature), his physical appearance (outer decay mirroring Emma's inner moral decay), his song (mocking Emma's expectations of love).
(2) Ironic uses of idea of fate. Both Rodolphe and Léon use it as a way of suggesting to Emma that she is meant for them (Part II, Chapter 8; Part III, Chapter 1). Charles uses it here as a let out, a way of blaming neither himself nor Rodolphe.

Are the characters to blame?
Perhaps some evidence for this in Flaubert's treatment of Emma (she is

'punished' for her adultery) and more so in the case of Rodolphe (Flaubert presents him as a villain, implying moral condemnation and blame). But . . .

Fate as determinism:

(1) Charles. Predominantly psychological determinism: given certain characteristics (Part I, Chapter 1), he never changes but is pushed into doing things (by his mother, Emma and Homais).

(2) Emma. A combination of psychological determinism: 'tempérament plus sentimentale qu'artiste' (more of a sentimental than an artistic temperament), cultural determinism (her reading and religious experience, Part I, Chapter 6) and social determinism (society encourages her through glimpses of high living, Part I, Chapter 8, but restricts her as daughter of peasant farmer and as a woman, then closes in on her and destroys her, through Lheureux).

Conclusions:

To a large extent Charles's comment is not justified. The blind beggar clashes with the realistic register of the novel as a whole. But Charles's comment can be justified in part if we interpret fate as determinism. There is certainly very little evidence that the characters are free and hence possibly themselves to blame.

Sample essay or examination questions

(a) 'There are no isolated, gratuitous descriptions in my book; all serve my characters and have an immediate or long-term influence upon the action' (Flaubert). Discuss Flaubert's use of description in *Madame Bovary*.

In *Madame Bovary* Flaubert describes objects, people and places. Charles's hat is a typical object. Single individuals are often described in momentary poses, as Emma is while out walking with Léon (Part II, Chapter 3). There are also longer, much more varied descriptions of crowds, for example, at the wedding and at the agricultural show. Yonville is described in Chapter 1 of Part II, and Rouen as Emma arrives there by coach to visit Léon.

Even the evocation of Yonville, potentially the most isolated of these descriptions, is linked to what follows in the chapter: Flaubert's focus progressively narrows from the countryside to the village to the *Lion d'or* where Homais and Madame Lefrançois await the arrival of the new doctor and his wife. The description is certainly not gratuitous. Flaubert presents Yonville as a remote, dull place set in 'paysage sans caractère'. This setting will have a long-term influence on Emma Bovary. Most of the other descriptions are even more closely integrated with the action of the novel. The wedding scene, like the description of Yonville, shows Emma in the surroundings of a particular place and time. It allows us to experience what life was like in provincial Normandy in the early 1840s—so very different from the life Emma dreams of. The chapter describing the agricultural show develops this same contrast. Like the wedding scene, it depicts a slice of typical provincial life. Within that similar framework, however, it gives much more space to Emma. The action of the novel, the values and aspirations of its principal character, are thus set against the typical, and each comments on the other.

Very often in *Madame Bovary*, what is described is seen as if by the characters themselves. Léon, captivated, watches Emma pick her way on stepping stones through the mud; Emma observes life at Vaubyessard and implicitly compares the luxury and excitement she sees there with the dullness of her own existence. The picture of Rouen revealed to Emma from the *Hirondelle* conveys her excited anticipation and perhaps also her foreboding: the passage concludes with an image of destruction, with airy waves breaking against a cliff. Such descriptions tell us directly about the characters. They do not so much influence the action as become part of it. No French novelist before Flaubert had used description in quite this way.

(b) Discuss the view that in *Madame Bovary* Flaubert's aim is 'to study clinically the disease of Romanticism' (E. Starkie).

The key words in this question are 'clinically', 'disease' and 'Romanticism'. Since the author of the quotation is provided, the opportunity exists to track this quotation to its source, at least in the case of a term essay. It is very good practice to do so because seeing the context in which a statement is made helps to explain it. Of course the author's ideas have to be developed and new examples found. This particular judgement is made on page 297 of Dr Starkie's book *Flaubert, the Making of the Master*, listed in the bibliography at the end of these Notes.

This question is largely about Emma and the way Flaubert presents her. One might begin by considering what is Romantic about Emma, about how she thinks and how she acts. The capital letter at the beginning of 'Romanticism' suggests that Romanticism is thought of here as a specific historical movement. If the subject is set as a term essay, it would be well to seek help from a history of literature or from a teacher or tutor. An alternative would be to re-read Part 3 of these Notes which deals precisely with this subject.

The second part of the question concerns Romanticism as a disease. One can take this to mean: does Flaubert present Emma critically, as someone who has been corrupted by what she has read, by a climate of ideas and feelings which make it impossible for her to adjust to life in the real world? At this point, comparison with Charles and Léon might be appropriate since they show traces of the same influences. One might eventually want to question the truth of the statement. Is there not something to be said in favour of Romanticism, especially when one sees the values and actions of those who have no trace of it in their veins?

The word 'clinically' suggests that Flaubert writes in a detached and precise way, like a surgeon using a scalpel. Parts of the description of Emma's death could be used to illustrate how coolly precise Flaubert can be and how sparsely he uses explicit comments. On the other hand, does his sometimes lyrical tone not suggest that the apparently detached, ironical observer is in fact deeply attached to his heroine? And is 'clinical' the right word to apply, for example, to Emma's conversation with Léon when she arrives at the *Lion d'or*? Few surgeons operate with such a broad smile on their lips.

Part 5

Suggestions for further reading

The text

(a) in French:
Madame Bovary, edited by B. Ajac, Garnier-Flammarion, Paris, 1986.
The detailed notes at the end of Ajac's edition will be found to complement those in Part 2 of this book.
Oeuvres, edited by R. Dumesnil, Bibliothèque de la Pléiade, Paris, 1966.
The introduction to this edition gives Maxime Du Camp's account of how *Madame Bovary* came to be written (pp.12–13).
(b) in English:
Madame Bovary, translated by A. Russell, Penguin Books, Harmondsworth, 1950.

Flaubert's correspondence

(a) in French:
Les Oeuvres de Gustave Flaubert, edited by M. Nadeau, Editions Rencontres, Lausanne, 1964–67. Vol. 7, *Correspondence 1853-6, La Genèse de 'Madame Bovary'*; and Vol. 12, *Correspondence 1865-70, À propos de 'L'Education sentimentale'*. The first of these volumes contains letters to Louise Colet and Louis Bouilhet, the second, letters to George Sand quoted in these Notes.
(b) in English:
Gustave Flaubert, *Letters*, edited by F. Steegmuller, Faber, London, 1982. Vol. 1, 1830–56; Vol. 2, 1857–80.

Flaubert's life

BARNES, J.: *Flaubert's Parrot,* Picador Books, London, 1985. Not a biography, but a novel about a man trying to reconstruct Flaubert's life. Fragmentary, therefore, but also accurate and very amusing.
BART, B.: *Flaubert*, Syracuse University Press, Syracuse, 1967. Well

informed and discusses *Madame Bovary* at length, including an account of its origins and writing.

STARKIE, E.: *Flaubert, the Making of the Master*, Weidenfeld and Nicolson, London, 1967. Deals with Flaubert's life up to the time of *Madame Bovary*.

Criticism

BARNES, H.: *Sartre and Flaubert*, Chicago University Press, Chicago, 1981. A very lucid account of Sartre's view of Flaubert. Chapter 9, pp.340–87 is on *Madame Bovary*. The view of Emma taken in these Notes is based on pp. 343–4.

BROMBERT, V.: *The Novels of Flaubert: A Study of Themes and Techniques*, Princeton University Press, Princeton, 1966. The chapter on *Madame Bovary* is an excellent study of patterns of themes and images.

JAMES, H.: 'Gustave Flaubert, 1902' in *Selected Literary Criticism*, Heinemann, London, 1963, pp. 212–39. Set the tone for much Anglo-American criticism of Flaubert: praises him as a craftsman, but has reservations about the adequacy and interest of his characters.

SHERRINGTON, R.J.: *Three Novels by Flaubert*, Clarendon Press, Oxford, 1970. By emphasising Flaubert's use of subjective points of view, provides a good key to the themes, characters and unity of *Madame Bovary*.

THIBAUDET, A.: *Flaubert*, Plon, Paris, 1922. The first classic study of Flaubert. Worth consulting on Flaubert's style, Chapter 10.

Other texts

BALZAC, H. DE: *Old Goriot*, translated by M.A. Crawford, Penguin Classics, Harmondsworth, 1951.

CHATEAUBRIAND, F.-R. DE: *Atala, René*, Garnier-Flammarion, Paris, 1964.

The author of these notes

ALASTAIR B. DUNCAN is a lecturer in French at the University of Stirling. He has also taught at the Universities of Reading and Haute Bretagne, Rennes. His publications are mainly in the field of the French New Novel, especially on Claude Simon.